8.95

For Susan,
I look forward to
working with you!

The Darkness Beneath All Things

ERIC GREENWAY

Eric Greenway

HAGIOS PRESS

Library and Archives Canada Cataloguing in Publication

Greenway, Eric, 1953-
The darkness beneath all things / Eric Greenway.

ISBN 0-9735567-5-7

I. Title.
PS8613.R443D37 2005 C813'.6 C2005-904963-4

Edited by Harriet Richards.
Designed and typeset by Donald Ward.
Cover design by Yves Noblet.
Cover art: *Valley Eclipse* by Chris Lynn, courtesy of Garry Thurber, Letterbox Gallery, Lumsden; photograph by Zach Hauser.
Set in ITC Galliard and printed on 100 per cent post-consumer recycled paper. Printed and bound in Canada.

The publishers gratefully acknowledge the assistance of the Saskatchewan Arts Board, The Canada Council for the Arts, and the Cultural Industries Development Fund (Saskatchewan Department of Culture, Youth & Recreation) in the production of this book.

HAGIOS PRESS
Box 33024 Cathedral PO
Regina SK S4T 7X2

For Donna, Adrienne, Stephanie, and Madeleine

Contents

The House of the Lamp

IN THE BRIGHT OVAL CAST BY THE CAR'S HEADLIGHTS, DELICATE fingers of snow drifted across the charcoal expanse of Highway 2 north. David watched the road carefully, resisting the seductive pull of the snow toward the shoulder, his eyes on the painted lines that marked his lane.

Alone in the car, in this small universe of light and motion, he could believe that his life in the city did not exist. This was a lucid dream without voices and colour — only the even, low sounds of the motor and the silent internal bleeding of his thoughts.

He had driven this highway with Susan many times. When they were first together, they often drove in silence, the scattered stars and farm lights piercing in close around them. She would lean across to him and slip her fingers between the buttons of his shirt, and watch his face. The journey seemed long then, the mended sheets and sagging mattress at his parents' house unbearably distant.

More recently, they would begin to talk as they neared the farm — about her family, the economy, the novel he was teaching his high school students. He knew now what he could not admit then — that it was a pretense, a rehearsal for the parts they'd play for his parents. And perhaps for themselves as well, a last defence for the fast-eroding island of their common ground.

Six weeks had passed since the Saturday she'd packed her clothes in luggage he'd never seen before and stood in the doorway looking back.

"Just let it go, David," she'd said. "It's not like there's anything left, so why pretend?"

He hadn't spoken for several moments. The space between them stretched tight and perilous as a highwire.

"I can't believe this is happening," he said finally. "After five years, you can just walk away."

He turned his back and looked out across the street at an apartment building identical to the one they stood in, balconies and windows a mirror image of their own.

"You've been walking away for years," she said. "I'm tired of watching it happen. I'm tired of living that way."

"It can change," he insisted, doubting his words.

"It's too late for that, David." He heard the rattle of keys being hung by the door. Then in a voice that was controlled, kind: "I'll call you about the furniture and the rest of it. Take care of yourself."

A SIGN LOOMED GREEN out of the darkness, and he braked and turned to the right. The road was narrower now. In places drifts lay across his path — thick, hard snakes of snow that thumped against the tires and jerked the steering wheel in his hands.

For weeks, he had said nothing. Then in the staff room one day, a colleague asked about Susan, and he told him. The crowded room was suddenly attentive, carefully sympathetic.

"We thought you seemed quiet lately," someone said, "even more so than usual."

After that, he began to feel out of place with them. Susan had given him a way of belonging where he had never felt entirely at ease, entry into a world of social activities and endless, effortless conversations. Now he found himself overcome with awkwardness, like a visitor in a strange culture. He avoided those he had considered friends, leaving their messages unreturned.

He started to call his father more often. At first he intended to tell him of their separation, then found excuses for putting it off. He answered questions about Susan carefully and vaguely. But the deception troubled him. When they spoke, he began to picture his father standing stiffly at the phone, facing the wall. The loneliness of the farmhouse became almost palpable in his imagination, like the dust that had accumulated in the two years since his mother's death.

Perhaps that was why he'd suddenly decided to come tonight, despite the unsettled weather. Leaving behind a stack of rented videos, he'd packed some clothes, checked the trunk to make sure he had a snow shovel, and headed out of the city.

He hadn't been home since his mother's funeral; it had proved easier to avoid the dead than the dying. In her final weeks, after she'd been sent home from the hospital, he'd sat and watched her wither in her own bedroom. By the light filtered through the green roller shade on the window, their faces appeared grey and unnatural. She had always said that life on earth was fragile and temporary. The Bible verses she quoted and the hymns she sang around the house had reinforced that point of view. Now, instead of words, she seemed to be offering her own body as evidence, and for the first time, David was convinced.

HE TURNED ONTO the three miles of gravel that led to the farmyard. Even at night, the shape of the slopes beside the road, the position of the snowfence and the drifts were as familiar as the contours of his own body. He drove into the yard through ruts already half-filled with new-blown snow and into the circle of light from the porcelain fixture on the porch.

His father was surprised to see him, and pleased. He covered his pleasure by commenting on the foolishness of driving at night in March when a storm was brewing.

"Those shoes wouldn't do you much good if you got stranded," he pointed out. "And I don't suppose you've got a shovel either."

"I always carry one," David replied, sensing a small triumph.

He followed his father into the kitchen, waiting for the question he was sure would come. The room was large and uncluttered. The walls held only a calendar from a farm equipment dealer and a small framed print of praying hands. Warmth radiated from an enamelled coal stove that his mother had insisted on keeping after the gas had been installed. His father put the kettle on the range and brought the mugs and the instant coffee to the oilcloth-covered table. Then he poured the water into the cups and stirred in the coarse crystals.

"There's something I need to tell you," David said finally. "Susan moved out a few weeks ago. I guess things haven't been good between us for a long time. I'm sorry I didn't let you know sooner."

His father sat looking at his cup and stirring; his lips moved with his thoughts before they moved with his words.

"I thought it might be something like that, David," he said. He tapped the spoon carefully on the rim of the mug, then set it on the table before he looked up. "I see more than you think."

THE STORM CAME later in the night. David lay listening to the mourning of the wind in the eaves, the whisper of the snow blowing across the windows, and the slap of the power lines as they tugged at their moorings on the roof. The sounds of the storm and its nearness seemed to open a space within him, familiar but forgotten, like an underground cavern. It was a place of refuge, but filled with longing for something that was lost and irretrievable.

He awoke to a vigorous rattle from the kitchen. The day was clear and calm, the linoleum under his feet cold. He could hear the rhythmic half-turns of the grate as his father cleared the ashes from the firebox of the stove, then the heavy rumble of lumps of coal colliding together on top of the embers that had lasted the night.

When he came into the kitchen, his father was replacing the round cast iron lids over the firebox on the stove. He peered at David over the dark rims of his glasses.

"Sleep okay?"

"Yes, I did." David crossed the kitchen and glanced out the window. "Looks like we had some snow."

"Not much." His father stooped in front of the stove, pulled out a long, flat tray heaped with hot ashes, and emptied it carefully into a blackened metal pail. "It's been a warm winter — never seen it so warm this early."

"Here, I'll take that out," David offered. He could feel the heat of the ashes radiate to his hand as he lifted the pail and moved to the door. He stepped outside, and dumped the ashes in a pile by the caragana hedge. With an urgency brought on by the cold, he stopped to urinate in the snow, then laughed aloud at how quickly he went back to his old ways. When he went inside, his father was stirring oatmeal into a dented pot of boiling water. His movements were unhurried.

"Maybe you could set the table," he said. "The brown sugar's in the cupboard by the fridge there."

They ate in easy silence. The room glowed with the light reflected off the new snow, and the coal snapped in the stove behind them.

"I have to pull the pump out of the well today," he said. "Needs new seals. The way the sand gets in them, they never last for long."

David drank the last of his coffee and got up to help clear the table.

"Maybe you could take the cattle down to the dugout," his father went on. "They didn't get much to drink yesterday. Put a few bales in the half ton and water them down there. There's overalls hanging back by the door."

The overalls felt soft and slightly greasy to the touch. David pulled them on, then found some leather gloves and felt-lined boots. He went outside and drove the truck to the stack of feed.

His fingers seemed to find their own way under the strings of the greenfeed bales, and he lifted them with an ease that belied their weight. When the truck was loaded, he drove it out into the field, bellowing "so-boss" out the open window of the cab until the cows moved their gaze in his direction and began to trundle deliberately toward the truck. He steered through the snow in the direction of the dugout half a mile away, instinctively calculating the depth and hardness of the drifts, moving to the tops of the rises where the snow was blown shallow and accelerating through the soft depth of the hollows, feeling pleasure at the pull of the wheels against the drag of the snow.

Close to the dugout, on a flat space studded with frozen manure, he put the truck in first gear and turned the wheel hard to the left before hooking it in place with a rubber tarp strap. He let out the clutch, and as the truck began to circle slowly, he jumped out of the cab, and vaulted into the back. He tossed the bales off one by one, then he got behind the wheel again and stopped the truck in the centre of the circle. He walked unhurriedly to each of the bales in turn, sprang the feed loose from the loops of twine and spread it on the snow. The cattle crowded around him as he worked, and he spoke to them as he pushed past the coarse-haired bulging warmth of their bellies, his voice low and confident.

When he finished with the bales, he took the axe from the truck and walked to the dugout. A hole had been chopped through the thick ice several times that winter to allow the cattle to drink. The ice that had refrozen over the opening was yellowish in colour, and not as hard as the surrounding surface. He stripped off his gloves for a better grip on the axe, then began to swing it steadily, cleaning out the softer ice and widening the hole to form a trough large enough so several cows could drink at once. Fragments flew back and melted on his face as he worked.

A few cows moved closer, heads lowered, and watched intently for the first flow of water. After working for a few minutes, David put the axe down and knelt at the rim of the opening, reaching down to sweep out the larger chunks. At the bottom, the ice was thinner and dark blue. He stood up again, waved the cows back a few feet, then aimed a hard blow of the axe at the dark ice. The axe broke through, and as he pulled it free, water bubbled up and began to fill the hole.

Several of the closest cows moved forward to drink, and David stepped back to make room for them. More of them forced their way toward the water, and he remembered that they had had nothing to drink the day before. Further back, some of the animals raised their heads from the feed and began to move steadily and single-mindedly toward the dugout, stepping down over the shallow bank and onto the surface of the ice.

Suddenly, he felt the ice tilt under his feet. There was a creaking, groaning sound, then a sharp crack that came as a hard tremor through his legs. A hoof scraped on ice, and a few yards away, a cow dropped out of sight behind another. Through the herd, he glimpsed a thick, upthrust edge of broken ice, and black water. A cow was in the water, its hindquarters submerged and its front hooves scrambling for a hold on the slippery edge.

Several cows pushed toward the breach in the ice, curious and thirsty. David yelled and ran toward them. He swung his arms, trying to chase them back. His feet slipped, and he half fell, coming down heavily on the hand that held the axe. When he scrambled up, his hand was wet. A shallow flow of water was coming back across the ice.

He turned and made for the shore. Behind him, he heard another crack and a splash. A cow bellowed hoarsely.

He reached solid ground and looked back. Already, three more cows had broken through. Incredibly, others still moved toward the open water, insensible to the danger. A section of ice around the break began to sink under their weight, and then gave way.

David ran for the truck. He threw himself behind the wheel, started the motor, and revved the truck into motion. He built up speed on the level, then headed up a snow-covered slope, wheels spinning. His mind was calm now, empty of all but the truck, the farmyard ahead, and the path to the pumphouse where his father would be.

He flung open the door to the low building.

"The ice broke," he panted, lungs aching with the words. "We've got cattle in the water."

His father's face tightened, and he seemed to freeze momentarily. He dropped his wrench on the wooden planks of the well cover and sprang to his feet.

"Go phone Fred," he said, moving toward the door as he spoke. "Tell him to bring his tractor. And a long chain. I'll drive my tractor. Grab the chain by the back door and throw it in the truck. Meet me at the dugout."

In the house, David dialled their nearest neighbour without stopping to think of the number. He cut off Fred's drawled greeting.

"Can you bring your tractor and chains — some cows broke through the dugout close to home."

"I'm on my way. I'll meet you there."

David found a heavy chain bunched together on the landing at the back door and threw it into the box of the truck. By the time he got back to the dugout, his father was pulling up with the tractor.

The break in the ice was wider now. Twenty cows swam sluggishly in the black water, close together. The scene was strangely calm. Half of the herd had returned to the feed, their thirst satisfied. One of the cows in the water threw a hoof out onto the unbroken ice and heaved upward. The edge broke off, and the cow fell back, momentarily going under, then surfacing. She snorted, and shook her head vigorously from side to side, stretching her neck high to keep her muzzle clear of the choppy waves.

His father backed the tractor toward the dugout, and David brought the chain.

"Try to get the closest ones," his father yelled above the noise of the motor. "Loop it around their necks, tight enough so it doesn't slip over their heads. Be careful."

David hooked one end of the chain to the tractor hitch and pulled the free end toward the dugout. There was a shelf of unbroken ice between the level ground and the open water, and he stepped out gingerly onto it. A white-faced cow swam close to him. With one hand he pulled the chain taut so that the tractor supported his weight, and he leaned out to grab one of the cow's horns with the other hand. He pulled its head up on the edge, and knelt next to it. He dropped the end of the chain over its neck behind its horns, then leaned forward, reaching blindly under its neck to try to snag the other end. The cow began to pull back, and he felt a surge of panic.

"Hold still, dammit!"

He could hear the fear in his voice, and he struggled to remain calm. He pulled the cow's head closer, then made another grab for the chain. He felt his hand go underwater, fumbled for a moment, then found the loose end and drew it up around the cow's neck. He tightened the loop, and fixed the hook securely into one of the links.

He stepped back onto solid ground, and held the chain tight while the tractor inched forward to take up the slack. The chain grew rigid, and David moved back a few yards. The cow's eyes bulged as she felt the pull of the tractor. Her neck stretched out, and for a moment, David feared that the force was too much, that her neck would break or that her muscles would tear. But her front hooves came out on the edge and took hold and she thrust her weight upward. Her body began to emerge from the water, and as the tractor dragged her forward, her back hooves caught the edge and she was out, staggering toward the tractor as it came to a stop.

David set the cow loose and slapped its side. The cow walked past the tractor toward the herd, seemingly unhurt. He felt a rush of relief, and at the same moment, was overwhelmed at the number of animals yet to be saved. As he began to pull the chain back toward the water, he saw Fred's tractor appear over the rise. By the time David had hooked onto a second cow, Fred had backed his tractor toward the opposite side of the dugout.

"I'll be right there," he shouted across to Fred. He signalled his father to drive forward. When he was certain that the chain was secure, he waved to his father, and headed for the other side of the dugout. Fred was bent over the hitch of his tractor.

"I'll hook them on the best I can," David said, "and you can drive. If you can release them once they're out, that'll give me more time to work both sides."

Fred nodded and looked at the animals in the water. His face was creased with worry.

David dragged the free end of Fred's chain to the edge of the ice. A cow pushed its head above the surface of the water, snorting, just out of reach. He called to it, reaching out over the water, and it swam closer. He grabbed its horns, and sensing the danger in the animal's weight, he heaved back, drawing it toward him, then looped the chain around its neck.

After they'd rescued the first few cows, it became harder to reach the ones that remained. David ventured farther out on the ice to get closer to them. A cow thrust its muzzle up onto the rim, and he rushed to reach her, dragging the chain with him. But she drew back, and swam away from him. He watched in frustration for a moment, then the cow approached the edge again, a few feet farther on. David leaped toward her, but his boots slipped sideways on the ice, and he went down. He felt the brutal cold of the water as one foot went in, and the sharp rim of the ice across his hip. Then his weight came against the pull of the chain, and he yanked himself to safety and regained his feet. He looked toward the tractor, and heard Fred shout but couldn't make out his words. David waved, and turned back to his work.

He was cautious after that, his movements more deliberate. Each time he managed to catch hold of a cow and secure the chain around its neck, he grew more confident. When he leaned out over the water, he learned to take support from the back of a swimming cow, then to seize the moment when its head and neck came close enough to be encircled by the chain. His gloves were soon soaked and useless. His hands were red and numb with cold, and his knuckles bloody from the chain. Whenever he could, he thrust his hands into his pockets to keep them from freezing. Fred and his father offered to spell him off, but he refused. It didn't seem right to him that Fred should risk his safety for someone else's cattle, and David knew that his father was more likely to slip than he was.

Despite the cold and the danger, he found himself marvelling at the brute strength of the cows. Each time as the chain tightened, their muscular necks strained against the relentless force of the tractor. Their hooves thrashed powerfully as they lunged up over the edge of the ice. When they were freed from the chain, they shook themselves and rejoined the herd that stood eating just a few yards away. Except for the water on their sides, frozen into icy armour, there was no sign of their ordeal.

Finally, there was only one cow left in the water, swimming aimlessly, too far out to be reached. Fred and his father came and stood with him, and they called out to the animal from the shore, their tone rough and commanding. Her heavy head sank lower. Her snorting became weaker and less frequent, the great heaves of her neck and sides began to subside. The men fell into silence as her eyes grew insensible and her nostrils sank below the surface. She convulsed desperately upward once more, then went under.

"Poor old Star," his father said. "We'll have to pull her out in the spring."

They turned their backs toward the dugout, and watched the herd.

"Could have been a lot worse," Fred observed. "Could have easily lost them all."

His father nodded. "I appreciate your help."

"You'll be okay getting them home?"

Fred shook his father's hand, then David's. He gathered up his ice-coated chain, climbed casually to the tractor seat, and waved as he drove off.

DAVID WAS AWAKE long into the night, listening to the muffled ticking of the house as it heated and cooled. His book lay open and neglected on the bed beside him. Fragments of the day's sensations returned to him vividly — the first movement of the ice under his feet, the sudden heavy impact of a falling animal, the desperate last breath of the drowning cow. He tried to dispel his memory of the water, just one misstep away, dark and treacherous and deadly.

He reached to turn off the reading lamp, then stopped, unwilling to face the darkness. The lamp was old and handmade. From the time of his earliest memories of this room, it had been hooked over the brown iron headboard. Someone, perhaps his father, had made the lamp by cutting a round hole in the bottom of an empty jam can and attaching an electrical socket through the opening. A Christmas card scene of a house on a snowy evening had been pasted around the can, and the windows of the house punched through with a nail, so that the light of the bulb shone out through their tiny panes.

He stared at the pinpoints of light, and the house of the lamp opened to his imagination. He thought of the room beyond the window, and the boy who lay in the room, the hard edge of a book on his chest, listening to the sounds of his house, and the low rise and fall of his parents' voices somewhere in the warm space they shared.

He longed for Susan tonight. He wanted to tell her the story of the day just past, about the dangers they'd faced, the tragedies they had somehow held at bay. He wanted the warmth of her there, the shape of her body fitted back against him as they watched the tiny glowing window where the boy lay.

IT WAS LATE MORNING when David awoke. Surprised at how long he'd slept, he got up quickly and made the bed, stretching the old woollen blankets until the edges were straight lines, parallel with the head of the bed. He dressed and packed his clothes, then carried his bag into the kitchen.

His father was sitting at the table, *Country Guide* open in front of him.

"I thought you'd be in church," David said.

"Doesn't hurt to miss at times, I suppose." A hint of a smile touched the corners of his father's mouth.

"I should go soon," David said, thinking of the videos to be returned. "I've got things I need to do this afternoon."

He poured cereal and milk into a bowl, and ate hurriedly. His father sat reading at the table, waiting for him to finish. The sounds of food and turning pages seemed unnaturally loud.

After breakfast, his father followed him to the car. David got in behind the wheel, and left the door open. His father stood in the opening, his arm resting on top of the door, his eyes turned away.

"We could have lost you yesterday," he said finally. He looked at David, and their eyes met briefly.

"I guess you're right," David replied. He felt that there should be more to say, but could think of nothing.

He started the car. His father reached forward, patted his shoulder, then let his hand rest there for a moment.

"Be careful on the road." He stepped back and swung the car door closed.

David raised his hand in a mute farewell, and drove along the rutted path that led out of the yard. When he reached the road, he stopped and glanced back. His father stood watching him, squinting into the light. Against the brilliant white of the new snow, he looked shrunken, weak, his shoulders rounded by work and time. David lifted his hand from the wheel and waved goodbye once more, and without waiting for a response, turned out onto the road and drove away.

Vultures, Bearing Gifts

BEFORE HE LIFTS THE BINOCULARS, PHILIP RECOGNIZES THE DIS-tinctive flight of the turkey vulture. The upward sweep of the wide, motionless wings, tips raised, reminds him of a figure skater with her arms stretched to the sides and fingers extended. Philip grins at the comparison, and for a moment pictures a skater in a vulture suit.

"Beautiful," he mutters. He admires the silver-grey flight feathers on the underside of the wings. "Beautiful. Except for that bloody ugly head."

He's transfixed by the red, naked head — impossible to look at without imagining it plunged into some rotting carcass. He sees it pivoting from side to side, eyes sweeping the ground. The motion seems calculated and mechanical, like an oscillating fan. Not at all like the easy grace of the bird's flight.

The vulture circles back toward him. "I'm the live one here," Philip says, and follows the bird with the binoculars.

He imagines the scene from the vulture's perspective. He'd appear to be a strange beast, head back and lips stretched over exposed teeth, standing on a bare hilltop that falls away to water on the south and west, the slopes dense with hazel and chokecherry. Rows of crosses throw sharp shadows against the dry grass. The creature in the cemetery has some sort of removable, oversized eyes that glint on the ends of black stalks.

The sweat under Philip's collar runs down his neck, trickles onto his back. It's hot, breathlessly hot. The circle of August sky around the vulture is cloudless, the palest of blues. A blow dryer of a west wind hisses up from the lake, pushes against him steadily. He hears a tractor in the distance. A great day to cut hay, and for burning up already sparse crops.

His neck begins to stiffen. He takes one hand from the glasses and reaches back to rub it as the vulture soars straight overhead.

A sudden wave of dizziness overtakes him, and he steps back to catch his balance. Where he expects solid ground, the surface tilts away under his foot and he lurches backward. The binoculars bang against his chest as he flings his arms outward. His heel is caught fast by something, and his foot twists to the side. Pain shoots up from his ankle, through his calf, rises to an unbearable crescendo. There's a snap like dry kindling, and he goes down, one leg turned under the other, the heel of his sandal wrenching free in a tortuous jerk.

He hears a croaking sob, feels the sound forcing its way through his throat. His head thrashes from side to side. He whimpers as the pain flows over him, and he loses consciousness.

IRREGULAR SHAPES loom and shift against the darkness. Blobs of colour form and reform, muted greens, yellows, blues. His head throbs, and something hard presses against the back of his skull, just above his neck.

Philip opens his eyes, and pain flares up at the onslaught of white. He keeps them open and the white becomes blue sky.

He's on his back, chin pressed hard into his chest. The earth seems to be clutching at him — no, swallowing him whole, shoulders first. He hears himself moan. He catches sight of a foot against the light. His own sandal, but above him somehow. His hips and legs — they seem detached but they must be his — are higher than his head and shoulders. He twists, and pain scorches him like a sudden engulfing flame. He closes his eyes against the nausea, feels the dry jaws of whatever monster has hold of him squeezing tighter. He wishes for darkness, that the damn thing would swallow him quick.

A small part of his awareness seems to step away from the pain and look back. There's no monster, just a shallow depression in the ground, little more than a foot deep. He struggles to bring a fragment of memory into focus — a storm, lightning, hard rain. Weeks ago. Afterwards, he found the caved-in grave, collapsed in on itself. That's where he's lying now.

Eyelids squeezed closed, he tries to map his pain, follows the river of black fire to its source. His hip, groin, and thigh are numb and aching. At the right knee, a sharper throb stabs through the dull undercurrent. And from his ankle, agony pulses out in every direction, crushing, brutal. He cries out again, and goes under.

HE PULLS HIMSELF into consciousness. An impulse nudges him, troubles him. He must do something. He tries out his good leg, glimpses the foot moving slightly. He pulls it toward him, lifts the knee. His calf has been resting on his other ankle — likely broken. With an effort, he moves the leg away from the injury.

A word forms in his thoughts and his lips purse. *Predicament.* A sentence comes together: *Philip, you've got yourself in a predicament.* He names the parts: *Fallen. Broken ankle.* He stops, considers. *Hot as hell.* His face is burning, and his legs too, from the cuff of his shorts on down. His hat is missing.

Something dark passes overhead.

"Not dead yet!" The words are audible. His mouth twists with hatred. "Black fucker."

That's no word for a good Lutheran. The thought teases him. *The only good Lutheran. . . .*

He's as good as dead, done for. He'll die lying here in the heat. How long before he'll be found? Long enough for the vultures?

"Oh Jesus Eleanor!" he says in one breath.

When had he said goodbye to her — yesterday? Her face flickers in front of him, then fades. The pain seems to subside a little, floats away from him. The earth is liquid now, hot and viscous as lava. He's sinking back into its black waves. He flings out his arms to save himself, and his right hand strikes something solid. He gropes, finds it again, hangs on.

"Eleanor," he whispers. He's got her by the ankle.

Rescue me. Before I go down for good.

But it's not Eleanor. He's alone. He's gripping something metallic, upright, solid. Something strangely cool in the heat of the day.

It's the cross that marks the grave. Aluminum. Always bright, always reflective. Never hot, even on a day like this. One of the crosses that Maurice made. Against his wishes.

"Bastard!" It's a blunt, guttural sound that burns in his throat. He sees Maurice's face now, wavering in the haze. And Maurice's eyes, pugnacious, overlarge behind his heavy-framed glasses. Philip grips the cross more tightly, and Maurice disappears.

THERE'S A SUDDEN RUSH of wind against his skin. He hears a sound like air through bellows. He feels a sharp edge cutting into his fingers, remembers the cross.

He opens his eyes. Something black looms at the far side of the cemetery, hunched toward him, barely thirty feet distant.

"Maurice." The name hisses through his dry lips.

How like a vulture Maurice has become! Or has the vulture become Maurice? Philip draws his free hand across his face. He shields his eyes from the sun and tries to bring the black shape into focus. The dark body wavers, turns its gaze toward him.

It's the vulture, poised on the corner post of the cemetery. No — it's Maurice, leaning against the fence, shoulders hunched into a lumpy black coat, collar high around his ears. Grey trousers below.

"Get away, you bastard!"

Weariness overcomes Philip, and he closes his eyes. He hears something — wind? Voices? He opens his eyes again, tries to blink away the sweat. There are more of them now — three, four — lined up, watching him. Conferring. Philip can't make out what they're saying.

The whole bloody committee.

Maurice has called a meeting of the cemetery committee. He can't be up to any good. They're all Catholic except for Philip, all of them with French names — Levesque, Garneau, Desjardin, Boucher — and all of them with ancestors in the cemetery. They know he joined just to keep an eye on Maurice, to remind Maurice that he held one trump card: Philip owns the land.

"It's mine!" he grunts toward the row of them. "Don't forget it's mine!"

They stir in their black clothes. He knows what Maurice will say, what he's always said. "My brother never should have sold it to you in the first place. Should have kept it in the family."

Should have, would have, could have — they don't count, Maurice!

The land is his, all eighty acres straddling the tiny lake, including the cemetery and the site for the cabin on the eastern slope up from the water.

I've got the deed to prove it!

He's had this conversation before, too many times. If they're listening now, they haven't shown any sign. They shift uncomfortably — dressed too warm for the heat. He tries to make out their faces against the bright sky. His eyes burn, sweat crawls across his forehead. They won't listen — they've never listened. If they had, he wouldn't be hanging onto one of Maurice's damned aluminum crosses now.

"Claptrap," he whispers. If he had the strength, he'd pull it out and wave it in their faces.

He closes his eyes. In the darkness, he hears them, shuffling their papers. Then he sees them too, moving closer in the gloom. Maurice is in the middle, and the rest of them crowd around, just behind him.

"Practicality," Maurice says, his head moving from side to side. "It's a simple matter of practicality. Wooden crosses rot. Wooden crosses are crooked. Any fool can see that. Stick out at every angle. Like bad dental work."

He stops to grin at Philip, baring his dentures.

"Replace them!" he crows, and the others begin to nod, their heads bobbing as if they're on strings. "I can make up new ones in the shop myself for a couple hundred bucks."

Philip tries to speak up. *You're tearing up history!* He can't get the words through his swollen throat. *Historical artifacts, handmade by next of kin.*

Maurice looms in the darkness.

"I'm a hell of a lot more next of kin than you are, *Johnson*, last time I looked at the names on those graves." He towers over Philip, then stretches his black arms out toward him. "And what these hands make is as handmade as the next guy's!"

Philip cringes, then recovers his nerve. *Claptrap! Sterile, impersonal, machine-produced claptrap!*

But Maurice has disappeared.

THE PAIN IN HIS ANKLE and knee has become a dull, constant ache, as if a vice is tightening on his right side and leg. His skin is burning fiercely. He feels sharp sudden pangs across his nose and forehead, and imagines that deep cracks are opening in his skin.

He needs his hat. It must have come loose when he went down, fallen behind him somewhere. He opens his eyes. The sun is still high, slightly to his right. He looks toward the fence. The vulture — or was there more than one? — is gone.

He presses his head back hard, strains the muscles of his neck, lifts his shoulders. He twists his head back to the right and the left. He spots his hat just over his left shoulder, crown side down. He rests a moment, then pushes himself up again, bracing his good heel into the sod for leverage. He reaches over and back with his right hand, and his fingers graze the felt brim. He lunges again, and he has it. Fresh pain stabs through his leg and forehead, his shoulders ache. He covers his face with the wide hat, and feels instant relief from his neck to his scalp. The shade clears his thoughts.

He knows the reprieve is temporary. At these temperatures, with the sun and the wind, he's dehydrating quickly. His only hope is that someone will come to visit the cemetery. But on a weekday, that's not likely.

He gropes for the base of the cross again, finds it, holds on. He feels reassured — it's the one thing that seems sure and unchanging. He thinks of Eleanor.

"Be careful out here," she said. "Help isn't that close by."

"I'll be fine," he said to her. They kissed, and she drove off to visit her sister in Southey.

He tries to remember Eleanor's face, that last kiss. He feels tears coming. He imagines her finding him here. A sob begins to constrict his chest.

Get a hold of yourself.

He traces the day's events — remembers cooking oatmeal, filling the hummingbird feeders. He shut all the windows tight against the heat, lowered the blinds, and turned on the fans. He remembers the feel of cucumber in his mouth — a cucumber and salmon sandwich for lunch, and a beer.

My soul for a beer.

Then the dishes. He'd put his hands in the dishwater, and felt a sudden urge to pee. He stepped out into the oven heat of midday and headed for a patch of bush rather than the outhouse. He stood scanning the sky, and spotted the vulture. Wanting a closer look, he went back for the binoculars, and climbed the path to the cemetery.

That was one, perhaps one-thirty. An hour ago, maybe two. Now it's the hottest time of day. He's weak. Most of the time, he can't seem to think straight. Can he just lie here until the sun goes down? And what then?

My soul for a cell phone. A beer and a cell phone.

He listens, but there are no takers.

HE HEARS THE WIND, then another sound. Air brushing against something, not the grass or the bushes. Something higher.

They're back. He hears them again — Maurice and the rest of them, scheming together in dry whispers, almost inaudible. They can't see him, he's almost sure of it. His hat has grown huge, covers him like a hot brown tent. He can see the light coming in at the bottom edges where it's pegged to the ground. He lies very still, tries to breathe quietly. If he listens, he can just make out their words.

Consecrated, one of them says.

Yes. Another voice. *Sacred.*

He stirs, begins to answer, then stifles the impulse. Forces himself to be still and silent. He strains to hear more, but they're disguising their voices, making them sound like the wind. But he knows, he knows what they're saying. What they're always saying.

Protestant. He hears that. *Separated brethren.*

It's a conspiracy — they're plotting against him. Don't want him to be buried in their consecrated ground. Can't stand the thought of his and Eleanor's graves polluting the unspoiled sameness of their sacred place. Want it to stay all Catholic, all French. Especially Maurice.

But it's mine, and I love it here. I take care of this place.

He holds his breath. Had he spoken aloud? They've stopped whispering.

His back aches. He's sunken lower, his body is deeply curved into an earthen hammock. It's like a resting place. That's all he wants, all he and Eleanor want. Here, overlooking the lake, on the land they love.

Resting place.

He starts. One of them has spoken, read his thoughts.

Yes. Resting place.

He's certain he heard a voice. Kinder now, reassuring.

Rest. Rest.

He feels relieved, grateful. They'll let him stay — they've agreed to grant his wish at last. Even Maurice.

No.

He's suddenly suspicious. Not Maurice. Maurice drives a hard bargain, never gives without getting more in return. Always has his own trump card hidden in his black vest.

Crafty Catholic bastard.

Philip hears him laughing quietly through his teeth. He's closing in. Desperate, Philip tries to get away. Something clutches him — or someone. One of theirs is below him — it's not just the living who are against him. It's wrapping him in its arms, black fragments of its rotting clothes falling away like feathers. He opens his mouth to scream. The base of the metal cross is still in his right hand — he yanks himself toward it. He twists, reaches with his left hand to get a better hold. He rolls on his side, and sudden light blinds him as his hat falls free. Pain rakes his body, like talons tearing away at his injured leg. He hears himself sob, then rushing air behind him and a sound like a rug being beaten rapidly, gently. He sees a flurry of shadows around him on the grass. He pulls himself up on his elbows, propels himself forward. He drags himself frantically away from the grave, and collapses against the ground, cringing. He looks back over his shoulder. The cemetery is empty.

He's lying face down on the level ground at the head of the grave. Except for his rapid breathing and low moans, everything is silent. He wonders where they have gone, then can't remember who was there. Blood pounds through his temples. He remembers his terror. His pulse slows. He's nauseated, dizzy, overwhelmingly weary. He rests his head on his forearms and closes his eyes.

THE WIND HAS DROPPED. The air is hot, but the sunlight seems less fierce against his back, its rays angled. He feels the strap of the binoculars around his neck. He pulls them off, gasps as the strap scrapes across the raw burn on the back of his neck. Pushes them aside. His hat is close by, and he reaches for it and places it on the back of his head. Rests again.

Something flashes, then becomes a steady, cold glint against a dark backdrop. He watches it — a light shining up from underground. He can't look away, struggles to focus. The light becomes a disk, metallic. A coin. A coin resting on the soil and flattened weeds in the lowest part of the caved-in grave.

Mine.

And Maurice and the others missed it. Watchful, rapacious Maurice. Hovering over the cemetery with a hungry eye, seeing everything, controlling everything. Except this one small coin. He missed this. Escaped his notice. And Philip would too.

He raises his head, glances over one shoulder and then the other. No one in sight. He shifts his weight to his good leg, digs his toe into the soil. Shoves himself forward, pivoting on his forearms.

Three inches.

He moves his arms ahead, one at a time. Finds a hold again with his foot. Pushes, grunting with pain. Rests.

"Maur-eess!" he whispers. He'll beat the bastard after all.

He pushes again, straining to lift his injured leg. The pain eases a little.

"Maur-eess!" His voice is a hiss of hatred and triumph, too quiet to be overheard. He's inching away from the grave. Too slow to be noticed. Stealthy. Hugging the ground, bent low as grass.

He wonders where they've gone — how far, when they'll be back. He sees the cemetery gate ahead of him, long yards away. It's open — he can slip through. He tries to hurry, but his leg drags across a pebble, and he whimpers. Rests again.

His nose itches and begins to run. He smells sage, sees the grey leaves crushed under his arms. A sneeze starts deep in his nasal passages, and he rubs his nose urgently across his arm to stifle the noise, leaving a muddy track. He glimpses a distant movement in the sky to the east, feels his pulse quicken.

"Maur-eess!" he whispers, and moves ahead, carefully, steadily. Now the ground slopes toward the gate, and it takes less effort to crawl. He tries to watch the sky, but sees nothing.

The gateposts are just ahead. He aims for the space between them. He craves rest, but he's almost there. Once he's outside the cemetery, maybe they won't be able to find him.

His shoulders come abreast of the gateposts, then his waist. A shadow moves, and for a moment he imagines Maurice clutching him by the ankles, dragging him back to the grave. He cries out and digs his fingers into the soil to propel himself forward more quickly. He thrusts with his leg, and his body shifts sideways. He loses balance and begins to roll, first onto his side, then heavily on his back.

HE'S AWARE at first only of sound, one sound — a low roar with variations in pitch. The sound seems to come from deep within him, as if he has become a large droning insect. The hard turf presses against his back, and he senses that his head is lower than his feet. The pain returns suddenly, as if he has forgotten to feel it for some time.

He opens his eyes. The shadows of the long grass and buffalo berry beside the cemetery path stretch out to the east. It's cooler. Maybe six o'clock.

He recognizes the sound. A tractor. Henry's. Henry is baling just across the lake.

He lifts his right shoulder, rolls onto his side, eases himself over onto his chest and arms. He flexes his good leg, braces the toe of his sandal against the ground. Breathes in, pushes, then exhales as he moves forward.

"Maur-eess," he hears himself saying.

For a moment, Philip seems to remember Maurice towering over him as he lay in the grave, his arms spread wide. Was it Maurice who knocked him down, abandoned him to die? If it wasn't, what has Maurice done to make him so angry? And where has he gone?

The cemetery path stretches down the slope ahead of him, twenty yards to the bottom.

"Maur-eess," he breathes, and moves forward.

He shivers. A cold tremor takes hold of him. The backs of his legs and neck are burning. His skin crawls. He sees bloody scratches on his forearms. The pain from his ankle and knee is everywhere, invades his gut, his groin, his hips. He's suddenly afraid of what the sun has done to him already — would he even know if he was dying?

And Maurice is to blame. He can't remember why, but he's sure of it. Philip crawls forward again. He imagines his pain as a flame of hatred, directs it toward Maurice. Rests. Tries to think of what's ahead of him.

He's close to the bottom of the cemetery path. From there, it's thirty yards on the level to the woodpile, maybe thirty more from the woodpile to the cabin. Inside the cabin, water. He licks his lips. His tongue is thick, sour. He feels a glimmer of resolve, pushes forward.

"Maur-eess."

He listens to the tractor. He pictures Henry perched on the seat of his old green Oliver, twisted back to watch the baler. So close. If he can reach the cabin before Henry leaves for town, he'll blow Eleanor's whistle to try to get his attention. After Henry shuts down the tractor, there'll be a few minutes of quiet before he drives away.

The pathway is steeper, and he crawls more quickly. But it's harder to ease the weight off his injured leg, and he cries out with the pain. At the bottom of the path, he stretches his arms out in front of him. He presses his face into the grass between his arms.

HE CAN'T HEAR the tractor, doesn't remember it shutting down. He lifts his face, listens. To the south, the empty box of a gravel truck chatters as it turns into the pit, a mile distant. Across the lake to the west, a cow bellows. But from Henry's field, nothing.

He rolls onto his side, then slowly pushes himself up into a sitting position. The shadow of the cemetery hill surrounds him now. The air is cooler, but his body still burns. The sun has scorched his buttocks through his cotton shorts — he feels the harsh abrasion of the dry grass beneath him.

There are dark patches across his vision. He blinks, and they drift and change shapes. He thinks of the distance to the woodpile behind him. How quickly he could get there on foot. He pushes down against the ground with both hands, lifts his weight off his buttocks, then skids backwards by propelling himself with his foot.

The manoeuvre seems familiar. He's moving like a baby, a baby who doesn't want to crawl on its hands and knees. He's helpless like a baby too, but with no one to turn to. He keeps moving.

At the woodpile, he stops to rest, resisting the craving to lie down. He tries to remember how far it is from here to the cabin, but he can't picture the path behind him, and it's too hard to turn around to look. The woodpile on his right is suddenly unfamiliar, and he's not sure that he knows where he is.

Despair rises in him like black flood water. "Eleanor," he whispers, and closes his eyes.

The darkness is cool and seems to offer solace. But something troubles him. At the edges of the gloom, shadows move. Against the silence, he hears a stealthy shuffling sound. Something is there, completely focused on him. Something with a name.

Maurice.

Philip cries out in panic, opens his eyes. His body is rigid. His fingers clutch at the dry grass.

He lurches into movement, pushing himself backward on his seat. He's fleeing from someone, but he doesn't know anymore where the threat is coming from. For a moment, he sees Maurice in the dim periphery of his vision, shrouded in black, his face and bald head flushed. But when Philip turns his head, he isn't there.

The trees on his right and left are deeply shadowed. Plenty of places to hide. The sunlight reaches only the tops of the aspens — they shine amber against the fading dusky blue of the sky. His shoulders burn with every movement. Tiny stones pierce the palms of his hands. Everything spins and tilts as if the ground beneath him is being flung about by a silent storm. A wisp of cloud glows pale pink in front of him. He struggles to bring it into focus, but it shifts away, fades.

After some time, he stops, perplexed. Under his hands, the surface has changed. He's sitting on something smooth. He sees wide, greyish stripes, separated by dark parallel lines. He touches one of the lines with his finger, discovers it to be a groove.

Boards — where have they come from? It's a floor of some kind, a wooden deck. He turns his head, lifts his gaze to the wall of the cabin, an arm's length to his right. He stares at the wall, then with an effort looks over his shoulder to find the doorway. In the fading light, everything seems drained of colour, familiar but changed. He edges toward the entrance, leans his shoulder against the jamb. A sensation he can't name rises through his chest and throat. There are tears on his cheeks.

He reaches above his head, finds the doorknob, twists it. The door gives against his weight, and he lifts himself across the threshold, seat first. He drags his legs across, swings them free of the door, and lets it close. Inside, the air is hot and stale.

On a stand behind the door, there is a plastic water container, its spigot just within reach. He leans back against the stand, opens the spigot to a dribble, and the water runs over his head, down his face, and onto his clothing. He finds the flow with his mouth, and the water fills the back of his throat. He tries to swallow, and begins to choke. A few drops trickle down his throat, then he gulps more of it. He raises his hands to the water, lets it run down his forearms, and splashes it across his face. The sweat and grit loosen and wash away. He gulps more, panting between swallows, then closes the spigot. He's exhausted. He slumps onto his side, and curls up in a pool of water that has formed on the tile floor. He shivers and closes his eyes.

WHERE HIS FACE RESTS against the back of his hand, there's a sticky wetness. He's drooling. For some time, he realizes, even while asleep, he has been thinking of food. His hunger is insistent, like someone shaking him into consciousness.

What he wants is a steak, baked potato, huge cobs of slippery salted corn. He remembers the box of granola bars in the bottom of the cupboard just a few feet away, close to the floor. He rolls onto his forearms, begins to crawl. His injured leg seems unbearably heavy, lifeless despite the pain. But his thoughts return to the food ahead.

Resting on one arm, he pulls the box from the cupboard and shakes out several bars on the floor. He picks up one, tears off the end of the wrapper with his teeth, and begins to eat. It's chewy and sweet. There's paper in his mouth too, but he's never eaten anything this good, with so many flavours. When he swallows, he imagines he can feel energy flowing into every part of his body. He bolts down several bars, then tries to plan his next moves.

Painkillers, he'll start there. They're in the medicine cabinet in the bedroom. He sits up on the floor, reaches to grasp the edge of the counter with both hands. He pulls himself upward, keeping his weight on his good leg. By the time he's on his feet, there's sweat on his forehead and he's dizzy again.

The interior of the cabin is dim, and he switches on the fluorescent light above the sink. He inches along the counter, supporting himself with his hands and hopping on his good leg. He rounds the stove, then spots the paddles for the canoe standing in the entranceway, in a five-gallon White Rose oil pail. He pulls one out, fits the wide end under his arm, and lets it take his weight. He hobbles forward on the makeshift crutch, away from the entrance and down the short hallway to the bedroom, using his free hand to steady himself against the wall.

In the bedroom, he reaches to open the medicine cabinet and catches sight of movement in the mirror. He sees a face, grimy and scabbed, for a moment unrecognizable. His skin is burnt to a dull red. His eyes are bloodshot, and his hair is tangled with grass and burrs.

"And the rest of you is worse," he mutters.

He finds the bottle of painkillers in the cabinet. A tube of ointment falls into the sink, and he stares at it, then remembers his burns and insect bites. He pushes the painkillers and the ointment into a pocket of his shorts. He shuffles out of the room, bobbing crookedly on the paddle. Already, he's tired from the effort of carrying the weight of his injured leg. He stops to rest, eyes his swollen ankle. It's ice he needs.

He negotiates the hallway, passes the outside doorway, and goes around the stove again. He follows the counter to the fridge and opens the freezer compartment. He reaches for a tray of ice, reconsiders, grabs a bag of frozen corn, and sets it on the counter. He closes the freezer door and opens the fridge. There are several bottles of water on the shelf inside the door. Eleanor's doing — he's never had much use for bottled water himself. Until now. He removes four of them and places them beside the vegetables. He closes the fridge and steadies himself against the counter.

His good leg trembles from the exertion. His armpit is sore where his weight came against the blade of the paddle. The pain from his ankle is sharp again. He takes the painkillers from his pocket, shakes four into his palm, and washes them down one by one with the bottled water.

The recliner is just a few feet distant across the room, but there's too much to carry for one trip. He picks up the bag of vegetables, hefts it, and tosses it toward the seat of the chair. He throws the first bottle of water and it bounces off the arm, hits the floor, and rolls under the couch. But the second and the third bottles land in the seat of the recliner and stay put.

He's tiring quickly, finds it difficult to think. He starts to push away from the counter, then stops, reaches to open a drawer. He rifles through spare batteries, plastic cutlery and empty bags to find a wide roll of masking tape. He pushes the roll over his wrist, takes a step away from the counter.

His weight shifts too far forward, and he hops frantically to regain his balance. The crutch drags on the carpet behind him, and he falls shoulder first into the chair. The paddle clatters onto the floor beside him.

"Shit," he moans, and hauls himself up onto the seat.

He tugs the frozen corn and the bottled water out from under him. He reaches for the lever on the side of the chair, and pulls it. A footrest pivots up from the front of the chair, pushing his feet off the floor. A grey bruise extends up his calf. He leans forward and settles the frozen vegetables gingerly onto the swelling. He tugs a handkerchief out of his pocket, opens one of the water bottles, and soaks it. He drinks the rest of the water, drops the empty on the floor, and places the wet cool cloth over his face. He reaches for the lever again, and the chair back reclines. He closes his eyes.

Something scratches against the roof, and he jerks into consciousness. *Maurice.* He listens intently, hears nothing but the wind. Weariness presses against him like a soft, dark weight, and he gives in.

WHEN PHILIP AWAKENS, the clock over the sink reads almost ten. He checks his ankle. The swelling has subsided under the bag of vegetables, but the bruising has spread farther up his leg. The pain is sharp, and he swallows more of the painkillers. Despite the heat of the room, shivers cross his shoulders and chest, and he removes the handkerchief from his forehead.

Through the patio doors on the lake side of the cabin, the sky is clear and the evening is bright with moonlight. If the weather stays clear, Henry's likely to be back to his baling tomorrow. But it's far from a sure thing. Even if he does return, will Philip be able to get his attention?

He feels more alone than he can remember — more in need of help and company than he's ever felt. He watches a distant yardlight for a moment, then thinks of the grid road just a quarter of a mile distant. Even at night, there's always traffic.

The roll of tape is still looped around his wrist. He moves the backrest to the upright position, and leans forward to remove the bag of corn from his ankle. He tears a strip of tape from the roll and begins to wrap it over his sock, starting just above his sandal and spiralling upward. He flinches with the pain, but wraps the tape tightly. He tears off more strips and builds up several layers.

When he's finished with the tape, he squeezes ointment from the tube and spreads it on the worst of his burns and insect bites. He lowers the footrest and reaches down to retrieve the paddle from the floor. He slides forward in the chair, and pushes to his feet, supporting himself with the paddle and the arm of the chair. He removes his hand from the chair, waits until he's sure of his balance, then takes a cautious step toward the counter.

He's stronger now, he's sure of it. He takes another step.

"You've got the hang of this," he says. "Just take her nice and slow."

He reaches the counter and rests against it. There is a thick oven mitt on a hook by the stove — he takes it down and tugs it over the blade of the paddle, then folds it over and fastens it with tape. He rummages through the drawer again, finds Eleanor's whistle, and loops it around his neck. He takes a small flashlight from the drawer, the size of his palm. He switches it on, tests its beam against the far wall, and thinks of the larger flashlight on the shelf by the outside door. He decides the small one will do, and sets it on the counter.

He'll need water, the painkillers, and something to eat. Maybe a flag of some kind to wave down a passing car. He opens another drawer, and finds an orange tea towel.

"Not enough pockets."

He's reassured by the sound of his voice — the same old growl. He's still himself, for whatever that's worth.

He slides along the counter to the fridge, takes out two bottles of water. He opens one and drinks, listening to the sounds it makes as it passes his throat and splashes into his stomach. In the freezer, he finds an unopened box of ice cream bars, and he feels a surge of excitement. He puts them on the counter with the tea towel and the remaining bottle of water.

He takes inventory: Whistle. Water. Flashlight. Ointment. Flag. Aspirin. Ice cream. Just the bug spray to pick up from the shelf by the door.

He loops the towel around his neck and knots it. He stuffs the flashlight in the pocket with the painkillers and the ointment. The water just fits into the other pocket, but it protrudes awkwardly. And no room left for the ice cream, or the bug spray.

He remembers his fishing vest. If he can just get to the entranceway where it hangs, it's got lots of pockets. He tears the flap of the ice cream box open, grips it in his teeth. The chill from the bars radiates to his lips and his nose, and he starts to drool. He can already smell the chocolate coating. He pushes himself away from the counter, then spots his watch by the sink and slips it on.

Ten-thirty. More than nine hours since he took his watch off. Nine hours of hell — and with any luck maybe just one more hour to go until he reaches the grid road.

He leans onto the paddle, tests the padding against his armpit. He edges away from the counter, hops one step. Another, and he's alongside the stove. His jaw begins to ache from gripping the box of ice-cream bars, but it's a discomfort he can live with.

How many in the box? he wonders. On his trek to the road, he'll stop to eat them at intervals to reward himself.

At the doorway, he rests against the wall while he pulls the fishing vest over each arm. He finds pockets for everything, except the last ice cream bar. He tears it open.

"Good job, Phil. Have some ice cream."

He gulps it down — tastes nuts, chocolate, toffee, ice cream. Thick chocolate-coloured saliva runs from his mouth and drips on his shirt.

The night air is pleasantly cool. He plans the route ahead. First the meadow path, then across to the access road. Past Henry's farm gate, the access road slopes uphill to the grid road. At the first headlights, he'll wave his flag and blow the whistle like a referee gone mad. Eleanor will be proud.

PHILIP REACHES the grid road at eleven-thirty. He steadies himself on the shoulder and unties the tea towel from his neck. He pulls the flashlight from a vest pocket, and grips the whistle in his teeth.

He frisks himself for ice cream, comes up empty. He checks the road both ways for traffic, sees nothing.

After ten minutes, headlights flash to the south. His grip tightens on the towel in his right hand and the flashlight in his left. The lights round the curve at the correction line a quarter-mile distant. He waits, anxious and suddenly exhausted, then starts to wave the shirt in the beam of the flashlight and blow long blasts on the whistle.

The lights come abreast, moving fast. The whistle shrieks and Philip feels fragments of gravel sting his face and bare legs. A pickup flashes by. He teeters, loses his balance, and falls backwards into the tall grass that slopes up from the ditch. He's on his back, the flashlight and the towel still in his hands. The air is heavy with dust, and it begins to settle on him.

The pickup slows — he hears it slide to a stop in the gravel. The motor idles, then the transmission whines as the truck begins to reverse. Desperately, Philip drapes the shirt over the paddle, hoists it above the grass, and catches it in the beam from the flashlight. The truck stops on the shoulder above him, and someone leans out the open window.

"What the hell?"

Philip knows that voice. It's Maurice, peering out from under the brim of his red baseball cap. His mouth is hanging open.

"That you, Phil? What're you doing out here this time of night?"

Philip lies back, closes his eyes. "I need a doctor," he says. "Broke my ankle — got a terrible sunstroke."

Maurice is kneeling in the ditch beside him, trying to get his arm under his shoulders. He lifts Philip to a sitting position.

"Take it easy," Philip moans. "My whole damn skin could peel off any second."

"Take it easy yourself, Phil." Maurice's voice is soothing. "We'll get you in to emergency in just a shake."

He loops Philip's arm over his shoulder, and helps him to his feet. Maurice staggers a little, and Philip catches his breath.

"Save the last dance for me," Maurice mutters.

They circle the pickup to the passenger door, and Maurice opens it. Philip backs onto the seat, and Maurice helps him swing his legs into the cab. Maurice pushes the door shut beside him.

Maurice gets into the driver's side and looks him over.

"Shit!" He shakes his head slowly, side to side, the peak of his red cap sweeping back and forth like a searchlight. "Phil, you look like shit!"

Philip leans back against the seat cushions, rests his shoulder against the door. "Maurice," he says, "you've never looked better yourself."

But he's not so sure — something about Maurice begins to trouble him. Maurice turns, peers out through the windshield, then hunches over the steering wheel as he puts the truck into gear. In the dim light from the dashboard, his coat looks black.

"Wait," Philip says, and the peak of Maurice's cap pivots back toward him. "Just one more thing."

"Anything, buddy." Maurice peers at him. "What can I do for you?"

"Could you take off that cap, Maurice?"

Maurice eyes him quizzically for a moment, and shakes his head.

"Sure, Phil." He pulls the cap off, and shoves it onto the dashboard. "You're a strange one, Phil. Always been a strange one."

The truck starts to move, and Philip closes his eyes. He's drowsy, but he won't let himself sleep. His right hand touches something metallic — the door handle. He wraps his fingers around it, and holds on tight.

Everything Turns Toward the Light

IT WAS A PRETTY TOWN, BUT ONE THAT KEPT ITS ATTRACTIONS OBscured. Gabriel and Marian came upon it as most newcomers did — they rounded a curve in the highway that ran roughly northwest from Grande Prairie to Dawson Creek, and the community appeared before them on the right, sloping gently up the eastern side of the wide valley.

A dusty row of businesses lined the thoroughfare through town — a feed store, motels, a lumber yard, a tire shop, and gas stations. They were maintained only at a level of order and cleanliness that was needed for efficient functioning. The weeds had been cut, but the grass around the utility poles was long and seedy.

Gabriel turned their rented moving truck off the highway and onto the unpaved parking area of a gas station. He stepped down from the truck, and went in to ask directions to the church. A middle-aged man in oily coveralls eyed Gabriel curiously as he took out a paper and pen to jot down what he said.

"So you must be the new pastor," he commented when Gabriel thanked him and was about to leave.

"Yes, I am," Gabriel replied. "Are you a part of the congregation?"

He shook his head. "Not much of a churchgoer myself. Rather be outside somewhere on a Sunday morning. No offence, Pastor."

Where a single traffic light marked the highway's intersection with Main Street, they turned toward the centre of town. In contrast with the view along the highway, the sidewalks in front of the pharmacies, grocery stores, restaurants, and hardware stores looked freshly swept, and concrete planters at the corners of each block spilled over with vividly coloured petunias. They followed the street uphill, until the business area began to give way to pleasant residential neighbourhoods, with large shade trees and well-kept homes.

The Peace Bible Church was located just off Main Street. The building was simple and steep-roofed, with white siding and arched windows of clear glass. They stopped the truck, found the double doors unlocked, and went in. The interior was cool, and smelled faintly of furniture polish and paint. The hardwood floors creaked as they walked up the aisle. Marian eased into a pew near the front, and Gabriel slid in beside her. He looped an arm around her shoulder.

"Here we are," he said, and felt his words were inadequate to the occasion. "This is what we've wanted for a long time. This is what we've been working toward. Our first church."

"No, *your* first church," Marian said. "Not ours."

He was irritated at the shadow she had cast over what he'd thought was a perfect moment. "I want it to be yours too. Why can't it be yours?"

"I don't want it to be mine in that way," she said. She put her hand on his knee. "I'm happy to be here, but my life is about other things, especially now."

The door opened behind them, and the room brightened. They heard a heavy step, and turned to see a broad-shouldered man striding toward them. He had thick black hair and bushy eyebrows, and a smile warmed his wide face.

Gabriel stood as he approached, and held out his hand.

"I'm Walter. And you must be Gabriel. Pastor Gabriel. It's great to have you here in the flesh. Welcome, Pastor."

Walter paused, still smiling, and watched Marian pull herself to her feet. "And Mrs. Pastor too." His gaze took in her rounded figure, and he blushed. "And Baby Pastor." He laughed, rocking uncomfortably on his feet. "It's great to have all of you here."

"Marian, this is Walter Reimer," Gabriel said. "He's the chair of the board. I've talked to Walter a lot on the phone."

"Well." Walter pulled on the peak of his baseball cap. "I've got a crew waiting at the house. We'll get you settled in no time, and then the wife's got supper on."

Walter ushered them out of the pew and toward the door, his grin never fading. Gabriel found himself involuntarily mirroring Walter's smile. Walter's enthusiasm was infectious, and Gabriel felt a burst of satisfaction with himself. He was twenty-six, just out of seminary, and about to be a father. And now he had what he'd wanted for years — a congregation of his own.

MARIAN WAS PLEASED with the house. It was small and impeccable, with a second bedroom for the baby. To them, the neighbourhood was idyllic. They went for walks in the mild evenings of late summer and admired the gardens and flower beds. But the residents seemed to take the attractiveness of their properties for granted, and shrugged modestly at Marian's and Gabriel's compliments.

On a Monday afternoon soon after they'd moved in, Gabriel and Marian went to the hardware store downtown to pick out a new light fixture for the baby's room. When they had made their selection and approached the till, Walter was leaning against the counter. He greeted them enthusiastically.

"Looks like it's the preacher's day off," he said. "What you got there?"

"A new light for the baby's room," Gabriel told him. "We want one that comes down lower over the crib."

Gabriel took out his credit card, but the proprietor waved it away. "You can use that plastic if you like," he said. "But most people here just open an account. I'll send you a bill at the end of the month."

Gabriel hesitated, but put his wallet away. "Do I need to fill something out — a credit application?"

The man behind the counter laughed. "We know where to find you if we need to."

As they turned to leave, Walter stood upright and took a step toward them. "I'll come up and give you a hand with that," he said.

"Thanks — but I think I'd like to tackle it myself," Gabriel replied. "I've got a brand-new home repair book I need to put to use."

"A book you say?" He seemed surprised, mildly disdainful. "Never thought about learning something like that from a book. I suppose a person could do that. Come on — put the coffee on and I'll give you a hand."

"No," Gabriel said, more firmly. "I'm sure you've got lots of things to do, and I really would prefer to do this myself."

Walter shrugged, looked away. He continued to smile, but his face was drained of warmth. "Suit yourself," he said. "But don't come running to me when you get electrocuted."

"You should have taken him up on his offer," Marian said when they were outside.

Gabriel felt a surge of impatience. "You think I can't do it, that I really can't do anything practical?"

"Gabriel, that's not the point," she said. "It's a way he can get to know you, one way he can relate to you when there aren't a lot of other ways. You could have the sense to see that."

He was stung by her words. "It's my day off. I don't want to spend all of my time with these people."

"You're the one who took the job," she said. "Face it. In a place like this, that's a big part of what it means to be a pastor. You can't just keep your distance like you do with other people."

"And what does it mean to be a pastor's wife?" There was an angry edge to his words. "Do you want to live up to all of their expectations too? I haven't noticed that you've been eager to make these people your best friends."

She didn't reply, and they drove home in silence. The satisfaction Gabriel felt at having the last word was bitter, and the tension between them lingered throughout the day.

AS THE WEEKS PASSED, Gabriel felt that the congregation was becoming, if not fully accepting, at least more accustomed to his presence. That fall, he went moose hunting for the first time.

"We're coming by to pick you up tomorrow morning at five, Pastor," Walter said after church, clapping him on the shoulder. He looked back, grinning, at a small group of men knotted together in the church foyer. "Make sure you dress warm — and you better clear out some space in that freezer."

Moose hunting was nothing like Gabriel had imagined. Instead of long, silent hours in the bush, carefully reading the significance of tracks and broken twigs, it seemed they spent most of the day in the trucks, driving first on gravel roads, then taking to the cutlines, talking and glancing casually out the windows. At intervals, they would stop to eat or to drink coffee, but their talk was all of neighbours and farming and the evils of government. Sometime in mid-afternoon, an abrupt "We've got one" came over the CB radio in Walter's truck, and the mood of the men suddenly changed. Gabriel understood little of the intent of their hasty consultation, except that he and Walter's thirteen-year-old son were to walk noisily through the woods in the area where the moose had been spotted in hopes of flushing it out into the next cutline where the men waited with their guns.

Gabriel never saw the moose alive. Somewhere ahead he heard rifle fire, and shouting and laughter. When he and Walter's son finally emerged into the cutline, arms scratched and feet wet, one of the trucks was already backed up to where the young bull lay. Gabriel felt a thrill of excitement and revulsion at the sight of the animal, but the others were casual again.

"Not that great of a kill," Walter confided. "But it's better than eating beef."

The men stood around the animal while Gabriel became preoccupied with cleaning the mud from his boots. It was some time before he realized that they were discussing how the meat would be divided.

"It's his," Walter was insisting quietly.

Though his back was turned toward him, Gabriel could hear the curtness of his tone, and he saw the deeper red on the back of his neck.

"That's the way you see it, Walter," one of the others replied in a low voice, taking off his cap and putting it on again, adjusting it carefully with both hands. "What I'm saying is that we can all use the meat — and we don't even know if he's going to like it, do we?"

They seemed to notice that Gabriel was listening, and they fell silent.

"There's a couple pails in the truck," Walter said to him. "Why don't you walk back to where that creek crosses the cutline and see if you can bring us some water?"

When Gabriel returned with the water, his hands sore and shoulders aching, the carcass was quartered and wrapped in a tarpaulin in the back of Walter's truck. He put the pails on the tailgate, and the men started to wash their hands and their knives.

"We've all decided this one's yours," Walter grinned at him. "Should keep you fed all winter."

"Well, thanks." Gabriel raised his voice to take in all of them, feeling the colour rise in his face. "Marian will very much appreciate your generosity."

When Gabriel got into the truck, Walter looked across at him. "These guys," he said, shaking his head with disgust. "Some of these guys would let you starve to death, Pastor." He slammed the floor shift into gear, and the truck jerked into motion. "You'll find out soon enough," he went on with a scornful bark of laughter. "What I'd like to know is how they can say they love God when they don't love his servant. Hey? Tell me that."

Walter turned to look at him, and Gabriel held his gaze for a moment. Walter's face had reddened, and the blue eyes that he had found attractive for their warmth seemed cold and hard. Gabriel looked away in silence.

THE BABY WAS BORN on the first of December, a boy they named Emmanuel. They'd gone to the hospital in early morning, then sat and played cards for hours. Gabriel wrote the score for the game and the times of Marian's contractions on the same scrap of paper. After a couple of hours, the games slowed and the contractions intensified; by the time he had filled one side of the paper and turned it over, his only entries were contractions.

The labour was long and difficult. The weeks that followed the birth seemed overcast with weariness, with only an occasional sudden gleam of joy and wonder at the life of their son. Marian seemed listless, Gabriel thought. She'd cut her dark hair short and straight, and her face seemed wider, her mouth set impassively. When they made love, her nipples tasted of milk, and when he entered her, she felt slack and unfamiliar.

"Don't you feel anything any more?" he asked, slumping away from her, his breathing heavy and his penis wet and cold against his thigh.

"I'm sorry, Gabriel," she said. "I'm just so tired, and I keep listening for the baby."

"I wonder if it will ever be the same." He felt for her hand across the sheets.

She was silent for a moment. "Probably not." He thought her voice sounded resigned. "I guess we'll have to learn to adjust."

At church, the baby gave them a new area of common ground with the congregation, especially for Marian. The day at the hardware store when he had refused Walter's help, Gabriel had been hurt by Marian's criticism. But until the baby was born, she too was reserved with the parishioners, so he felt justified in dismissing her words. Now she was sought out after church, and they seemed to have won her over. Many held the baby, almost reverentially it seemed to Gabriel, but they touched Marian as well. He stood and shook hands as people filed past and made perfunctory comments about the service. She began to have long conversations with other women, and with them, her face was transparent, full of shy delight. She was free to be herself, and Gabriel resented and envied that. He felt left out.

WALTER BEGAN TO VISIT Gabriel regularly at his small office in the church. At first, Gabriel welcomed the break from the long drudgery of sermon preparation.

"Good morning, Pastor." Walter would grin, and toss his cap on the floor as he slumped into the turquoise leatherette chair across from Gabriel's desk. "How's she going?"

But the tone of Walter's visits began to change. One midwinter morning he leaned forward in his chair and fixed his eyes on Gabriel.

"It's just not happening, Pastor," he said, his look grim and calculating. "It's just not happening."

"What's not happening, Walter?"

Walter snorted softly. "If you have to ask, maybe that's part of the problem." His voice rose, edged with impatience. "The Spirit's not moving," he pronounced. "Oh, there's nothing wrong with the Holy Spirit — he just knows where he's not wanted."

Gabriel tried offering reason, then encouragement. But he was plagued with a growing sense of doubt. Should there be more? he wondered. He'd wanted to be in ministry since his teen years. He'd admired a youth pastor who was passionate about his calling and who encouraged Gabriel in that direction. He'd always envisioned leading a congregation of happy, involved people — preaching insightful sermons, giving wise direction to those who were struggling with life's difficulties. He imagined being the kind of pastor that people outside the church would find approachable. Until recently, he had been confident that he would succeed. When as part of his seminary studies he had interned at a church in the city, everyone seemed to think he had excelled. There he'd been one of a handful of pastoral staff, and success was judged by how well he spoke, administered programs, and related to people, especially by involving them as volunteers in the work of the church.

Now he felt misgivings. Perhaps Walter was right. Perhaps he was failing to make something happen that was crucial to the spirituality of the congregation — but he had no idea of where to start if he wanted to make a difference.

After each conversation with Walter, he felt an increasing weight of discouragement and helplessness settling on his shoulders. He began to dread hearing the sound of Walter's heavy footsteps across the creaking varnished floorboards of the church.

"Walter, I'm tired," he found himself saying one day, though he hadn't meant to let down his guard. "Some days I'm so discouraged I don't want to go on."

Walter eyed him, nodding slightly. Gabriel thought he seemed pleased.

"How's your prayer life?" he asked suddenly.

"Well, I guess it could always be better," Gabriel said. "It's hard, with the baby and the late nights and never enough sleep."

Walter thumped his big fist down on Gabriel's desk. "No excuses, Pastor." He leaned across, staring directly into Gabriel's eyes. "There's no excuses good enough for God."

Gabriel met his gaze for a moment. Walter's face was coloured deeply, his jaw clenched, his eyes dark and fervent.

AFTER A YEAR in the position, Gabriel concluded his report to the church board with a request for an evaluation of his performance. The request seemed to startle and amuse the elders.

"An evaluation!" one of them exclaimed. "You're doing fine, Pastor. Keep it up! How's that for an evaluation?"

“Not quite so many twelve-cylinder words in your sermons,” another offered, “and a few more pastoral visits.”

Walter cleared his throat, and the scattered laughter subsided. “How do you think you’re doing, Pastor?”

Gabriel selected his words carefully. “All things considered, I think it’s been a good year, although I’d be the first to admit there’s lots of room for improvement. What I’ve found most challenging is the amount of time it takes to do administration and office work, time that perhaps could be better spent with people.”

“And God,” Walter interjected.

“Yes,” Gabriel said, hearing the irritation in his own voice. “There’s never enough time for God.”

“I think what you need is a part-time secretary,” Walter said, “and I’ll make that a motion.”

“We don’t have any money to pay a secretary,” someone objected.

“Where’s your faith?” Walter replied. “Where’s your faith? Why don’t you just let God take care of the money?”

A week later, Walter’s daughter started coming into the church office every afternoon. Jessica had just finished high school the previous June, and as Walter saw it, she didn’t have any ambitions.

“She needs something to keep her out of trouble,” he said, “so she might as well make herself useful at the church.”

At first, Gabriel was angry that he had no say in Jessica’s hiring. But she was bright and energetic, and she was soon typing up his sermon notes and arranging his schedule. Unlike her father, Jessica’s face was narrow and fine featured, with fair skin that contrasted dramatically with dark auburn hair. Her green eyes were attentive and intelligent, and she spoke to him with a directness and clarity he thought was uncharacteristic of her age. After a month, he asked her to sit down in his office.

“I just wanted to tell you how pleased I am with your work,” he said. “For the first time, I feel almost on top of things, and it’s because of your help.”

"Thank you, Pastor." She blushed. "I like working here with you."

"You must have other plans — university?"

"Oh, no," she said, almost too casually, Gabriel thought. "I just want to stay home for a while."

As the weeks of early fall passed, the reserve they felt in each other's presence began to fade. Gabriel would ask for her opinions about church programs, and he was impressed by her insights into people. She seemed to see below the surface, and recognized the essential things about someone's strengths and character. He grew to trust her judgement about sermons as well.

"What's this one about?" she asked him, scanning the books and yellow legal pad spread out on his desk.

"I thought I'd do the feeding of the five thousand."

She wrinkled her nose.

"You don't like the feeding of the five thousand?"

"It's not that I don't like it," she replied. "But what more is there to say? The people are hungry, the little boy brings his lunch, and Jesus does a miracle. Everybody has lots to eat, and there's leftovers besides. What does that have to do with me?"

There was a playful challenge in her words. Gabriel smiled at her, and she returned his smile.

"I think you're leaving something out," he said. "What about those five thousand people? I think they had a lot more to do with it than you're giving them credit for."

She sat down across from him and her expression became serious. "What do you mean?"

"I don't know exactly," he said. "But the story has to be about more than Jesus doing a magic trick. I think it's about that group of people, their openness, their desire. Maybe they somehow created the conditions where something amazing could happen, something that seemed completely beyond themselves."

She was silent. She reached up and pushed her hair behind her ear.

"Do you think I'm off base?" he said after a moment.

She shook her head. "No. Not at all. You could be right. But I've just never thought about it that way before."

Each day when he returned to the church after lunch, he found himself looking forward to her arrival. She would call out a greeting as she came in, and he could hear her hanging up her coat. Then she would come into his office to see whether there was coffee, and she would ask how he was. When she crossed behind his chair for the coffee pot, she often rested her hand lightly on his shoulder for a moment as she passed. He began to look forward to her touch; he told himself it was a sign of trust. On the days she didn't touch him, his disappointment was keen.

Some days she was effervescent and cheerful, and at other times she made no attempt to mask the darkness of her mood. One afternoon in early November when Gabriel's appointment had been cancelled, she seemed reluctant to leave his office.

"Is there something you want to talk to me about?" Gabriel asked her. "You seem pensive."

"Pensive?" She smiled ironically, then her smile faded and she looked away. "Bloody depressed is more like it."

The force of her words surprised him. "Do you want to talk to me?"

She hesitated. "I don't think so," she said. "Maybe."

She sat on the edge of the turquoise chair. "I wouldn't know what to say. I wouldn't know where to start." She sat in silence for a moment, and as Gabriel watched, a change came over her, as if a disguise had been lifted, her poise replaced by a weary vulnerability.

There was a sound outside the office, and Walter was suddenly framed in the doorway. Jessica leapt to her feet, her hand at her throat.

"Hard at it, are we?" Walter said.

"Didn't hear you come in, Walter," Gabriel replied. "Jessica and I don't often have a chance to talk."

He looked at Jessica. The colour had drained from her face, and her expression seemed frozen. Her lips were parted slightly and her eyes were wide. Gabriel laughed. "I think you've given your daughter a bit of a shock."

"Caught you two talking about me, have I?" Walter punched Jessica playfully on the arm. He glanced at her, then looked back at Gabriel. "Well, best be going. Some of us have work to do."

After he left, Jessica remained standing in Gabriel's office, turned partially away from him in the direction of her father's departure.

"How does he do it?" she said finally, her voice strained.

"How does he do what?"

"Nothing," she said. She shook her head, and turned to face him. "Can I go? I'm not feeling too well."

"Of course." Gabriel followed her as she went to get her coat. "Could you come with me tomorrow when I go to visit Annie Friesen?" he asked. "I think she'd be more comfortable if I had a woman with me."

She glanced at him and nodded briefly.

"Thanks for not calling me a girl," she said with a wan smile.

"You're not that much younger than I am," he replied. "Marian's just five years older than you are."

She seemed surprised, then thoughtful.

"And while we're on the topic," he said, "I think it's time you just called me Gabriel, at least when we're here by ourselves."

She smiled again, with more pleasure this time. "Sure thing, Reverend."

"Get out of here," he said. "You're supposed to be sick."

She laughed and turned to the door. "See you tomorrow, Gabriel."

When she was gone, he sat at his desk without working. The church building around him felt large and empty — in her absence the space seemed drained of vitality. He thought about how anxious she had been in the presence of her father, and her response puzzled him. He was eager to continue the conversation, but his eagerness was tempered with disquiet.

ON THE WAY BACK from the Friesen farm, Gabriel pulled up to the drive-through window at the town's only fast food restaurant. "Let's grab a coffee before we go back to work," he suggested, and Jessica agreed. He parked the car, leaving the motor running for warmth, then turned to her.

"We have a conversation to finish."

She glanced at him anxiously. "Not here, okay?" she said. "I can't talk here. There's too many people around. Let's drive out of town somewhere."

He turned onto the highway, then took a side road. She sipped nervously at her styrofoam cup as he drove, and he felt the tension rising between them. A few minutes from town, he followed a driveway that led through trees to an abandoned farmsite and stopped the car.

"This okay?"

She nodded. She set her coffee carefully in the cup holder between them, and stared straight ahead, her hands on her knees.

"I'd like to know what you were about to tell me yesterday," Gabriel said after a few minutes of silence. "When your father came in. And why you reacted the way you did."

"He startled me."

"No, it was more than that." Gabriel could feel her resistance. "You seemed afraid. I can't understand why."

She sat motionless. But she seemed to be calmer now, he thought. Focused, as if listening to something farther away.

"Yesterday, I was about to say what I've never said to anybody," she began. She glanced at him, then turned away. "It's that... I hate my father. I hate him. I want him out of my life. I'd be happy if he was dead."

She spoke precisely, and then paused. "That's what I was thinking. I was picturing him dead. Then suddenly he was there, as if somehow my evil thoughts had summoned him, and he caught me in the act. And inside he was laughing at me because I can't even keep my thoughts away from him."

Gabriel felt a wave of impatience. "Aren't you being a bit dramatic? Your father comes to my office almost every day. He happened to show up when you were thinking angry thoughts about him." Gabriel paused, shook his head abruptly. "And as for hating him, lots of kids think they hate their parents. I know I did at times. It's a natural part of the process of moving toward independence."

She turned quickly toward him, colour rising in her face. "Please don't patronize me. I know you're the adult here — you're supposed to have all the wisdom. But the least you can do is listen. This is my life. I've breathed every minute of it. And I know when something's screwed up."

He was taken aback by her anger. "I'm sorry," he said, feeling suddenly unsure of himself.

She picked up her coffee, drank, took a deep breath. "I'm sorry too. But you have to understand that this isn't just some adolescent bitch session. Maybe I take some of it too seriously — but it's serious to me, and I need to know you respect that."

"I do." He touched her forearm. "I'm sorry. Tell me why you say you hate your father."

"I don't know how well I can explain it. It doesn't always make sense to me." He watched her shoulders rise and fall. "I hate him because he wants me to live in fear. I hate him because he won't stop controlling me. I hate him because he makes me think and feel and do things I end up being ashamed of. I hate him because he wants to be the only one who knows what's true and says what's true, and no one can disagree with him."

She stopped, let out her breath in a long sigh, and drank from her coffee. "You say you're living in fear," Gabriel said after a moment. "What are you afraid of?"

She turned to him, shaking her head in exasperation. "That's just the thing," she said. "I don't know exactly."

"Is he abusive? Does he ever hit you?"

"Sure he hits me, sometimes. But not that often." She shrugged dismissively. "He slaps me once in a while. Nothing like what my little brother gets."

"But you're nineteen! Not that it would be appropriate at any age."

"I'm not saying I like it or that I think it's normal. I'm just saying that it's not what really matters."

"I think it matters." Gabriel was angry, and he tried to control the emotion in his voice. "And I certainly wouldn't be the only one."

She fell silent and turned partly away from him. The set of her jaw seemed stubborn and sullen, and he feared that she would end the conversation and never risk speaking to him again.

"Okay," he said. "You say his hitting you occasionally doesn't matter. Then what does? So far, that's the most concrete thing you've told me."

She turned to look at him, measuring him in some way. Her cup was empty, and she placed it carefully in the cup holder. "I'll tell you the concrete things if you want, but I'm not sure they're the whole story. One, he searches my room and my purse and my pockets. He does it while I'm not there and he tries to leave everything the way he found it. But I know, and he knows I know, and he doesn't care. He says the only reason I would care would be if I had something to hide."

She took a deep breath. "Two, he follows me and watches me. He might show up anywhere — like at a basketball tournament in Peace River, sitting in his truck across the street from the high school. I'll get up to leave the restaurant where I'm having coffee with my friends, and there he is in the next booth. If I talk to him, it's all very casual and friendly, but he wants me to know he's watching. Three, when I was in high school he read all my essays, every one of them. And then he'd tell me what was wrong with them, quoting the Bible verse that proved it. He'd grill me about what my teachers said, and then try to get me to tell him why they were wrong — 'expose their secular humanist presuppositions.' I actually got real good at that."

She smiled wanly at him. "How's that for concrete?"

He paused, turning his face partly away from her. Get away from him, he wanted to say. In different ways, this was the Walter he had come to know as well, and he doubted whether there could ever be a change. But she had come to him for help. What help would it be if all he could suggest was that she run away from the situation?

"Jessica, let me be the devil's advocate," he said finally. "Maybe your father has poor parenting skills, and he's a bit of a control freak. I can understand why you say you hate him. But other than his hitting you — which you say isn't the issue — I don't see much that's beyond bad parenting. Is there anything you're not saying?"

She was silent again. She traced patterns in the condensation on the car window beside her.

"Are you afraid he'll become more abusive, maybe more violent?"

She shook her head quickly, her forehead furrowed. "No, that's not what makes me afraid. Even at his worst, he's in control of himself. Even the time he knocked my brother down and chipped his tooth. He always says and does exactly what he intends. He never even swears."

"Then what?" Gabriel said. "Where's your fear coming from?"

With her fingertip, she filled in the outline of the square she'd traced on the window. Gabriel found himself thinking of the marks she'd leave, marks that would probably still be there in the spring.

"He seems to know things," Jessica began. "About a year ago, I had a really serious boyfriend. We talked about getting married. He was the first guy I slept with, the only guy I've slept with. The first time, I swear my father knew. He was waiting up for me, sitting in the dark as usual so he could surprise me. The first thing he says to me, before I even know he's there, is, 'Your body is the temple of the Holy Spirit.' Then he turns on the light and comes up really close, and asks me, 'So what have you been doing with his temple?'"

"He didn't necessarily know. Maybe it was your imagination, your guilty imagination."

"Could be." She laughed lightly. "Or maybe I smelled like sex. But it was very weird."

Gabriel swallowed uncomfortably, cleared his throat.

"I never admitted anything to him, but he was determined to break us up. After a while, I started to believe everything my father said about my boyfriend, about me, about the unhealthiness of our relationship. So I gave in. I'm not proud of it, but I couldn't take the heat. And it paid off — the day after we broke up, my father bought me my car. He told me I'd made him very happy, so I gave him a big hug and pretended I was happy too."

The car had become too warm, and Gabriel switched off the motor. "Is there more?" he asked. "You say he knows what you're thinking and doing. What else makes you afraid?"

"I'm going to get weirder," she said. "Things happen at our place — people say we're accident prone. Two years ago I'd been painting some granaries and I had the paint cans in the cab of the truck on my way home. I passed out from the fumes and rolled three times, almost killed myself. Last fall, my brother got buried alive in a bin of wheat. My mom saw his arm, and dug him out. One time, a bull we'd had for years turned on my father and smashed him through the corral fence. He broke a bunch of ribs and pierced a lung."

"But those are accidents!" Gabriel burst out. "Accidents happen! I don't know what you're trying to say. Your father probably got the worst of the three."

She pivoted toward him on the car seat. "I'm not trying to say anyone makes these things happen, especially not my father. I'm not that crazy."

"Then what are you trying to say?"

She coloured and looked tentative, but held his gaze. "I'm just saying that I think there's a connection."

"What? Do you mean to say you're jinxed? What is it?"

She didn't answer him at first. Gabriel looked out through the windshield. Everything was silent except for the sound of their breathing. He watched a few flakes of snow fall toward the frozen ground, and far off, against a bluff of bare trees, he saw a blackbird wheel and rise in the cold air.

"You said something once, about the feeding of the five thousand. You might not remember, but I do. You said that the people created the conditions where something could happen, something that was entirely beyond them."

"And that has something to do with this?"

"Sometimes you don't seem to know what you're saying, Gabriel. You think you're just playing with clever ideas, but then you say things that are amazing. Things that are really true. That was one of them. And it made me wonder, if people can create the conditions for good things to happen, unexplainable things — then maybe it's the same for things that aren't good."

He shook his head. "I think you're taking what I said out of context."

"I'm taking it out of the context of your sermon, the safe context of your sermon. But that doesn't mean what I'm saying isn't true."

He looked at her. There were times when her thinking seemed ahead of his.

"It's like there's all this dark stuff," she said. "Anger and chaos and destruction — just under the surface, just waiting to break out." She paused. "And then it does."

"Jessica," he felt himself shaking his head involuntarily, "I do care about what you feel. I care about what you're going through. But this... you're letting your fear get the best of you. What possible link could there be between a controlling, angry father and farm accidents?"

"Maybe you're right. But I think there could be. I thought maybe you'd know something about things like that."

The car was chilly. He started the motor and rested his hand on the gearshift. She seemed to notice his desire to end the conversation before he had acknowledged it himself.

"Have I said anything that makes sense to you?" she asked. She sounded fragile again, in need of his approval.

"I don't know. The stalking, the lack of respect for your privacy, the physical abuse — these seem to be the issues to me. But to be honest, I'm not sure I really understand your fear. What's the worst that could happen to you?"

"Damnation," she said quickly, then seemed surprised at her own response. "I'm afraid he'll damn me to hell."

"And you think he can do that?" Gabriel made no attempt to mask the incredulity in his voice.

"I don't *think* he can. But I *feel* that he can. I *fear* that he can. And whether it makes sense or not, it's working, isn't it? I'm living in some kind of hell now."

"That's what has to change."

"I want it to change. I can't live this way anymore."

Gabriel felt powerless, and suddenly anxious. "What do you want me to do? Do you want me to talk to him?"

"No. Maybe you're already doing it. Just listening. Asking questions. Making me think. Giving me some hope."

"Have I done that?" He turned to look at her.

"Oh, yes," she said. Her eyes were wet. She moved closer to him and rested her head on his shoulder. He found the gesture deeply moving, natural but unsettling. He touched her hair, and she closed her eyes. She reached for him, first tugging at the collar of his coat, and then her hand moved upward across his neck and his beard. He felt her fingertips brush across the curve of his lips. He stopped breathing, caught between the impulse to remove her hand or to press it against his mouth. And then she sat up, smiled at him, and the moment had passed.

HE WAS RESTLESS in bed that night, turning over Jessica's words in his thoughts. He told himself that she was overreacting, that time and independence would reconcile her differences with her father. But when he thought of his own relationship with Walter, how after even a few months he both feared and wanted to please him, he gave Jessica's feelings more credence.

Marian turned and drew him closer, but he pulled away from her kiss.

"Something wrong?" she whispered.

He hesitated, trying to find a way to begin. He felt he should be able to talk to Marian about Jessica — there was no one else he could talk to. But he was afraid of what he might reveal about himself if he did. He wanted Jessica to see him as more than her pastor and her boss. He wanted her admiration, her affection, her friendship. Admitting that to himself made him uneasy. In seminary classes, they had talked about the potential pitfalls of counsellor-client relationships, but it wasn't as easy now to say what was appropriate and what wasn't. Jessica wasn't a case study — she was a person he cared for. And she seemed to care for him too, regardless of his role. Could Marian understand what he was feeling, and could she accept it?

Emmanuel cried out, and Marian got up to take care of him. When she came back to bed, she moved close to him again.

"I've been thinking I should go visit my parents," she said. "Maybe for two or three weeks. I think it'll give us both a chance to catch up on our sleep, and they haven't seen that much of Emmanuel. I'll be back before his birthday."

"I wish I could come with you," he said. "But you know I can't."

"I wish you could too," she said against his chest.

He thought of Jessica again — her head on his shoulder in the car, the light incense of her perfume, and the strange cool touch of her fingertips against his mouth. He was sure now that Marian could never accept that kind of intimacy, no matter how innocent. He wasn't sure if he could himself.

WITH MARIAN'S DEPARTURE, he immersed himself in the work of the church with new energy. He arrived at his study early, and spent several hours in reading, prayer and sermon preparation before lunch. When Jessica arrived, he would hand her a list of tasks — volunteers to call, items for the weekly bulletin, appointments to arrange, committee minutes to type and distribute. Then he would spend his afternoons visiting members of the congregation in their homes and on their farms, or making contacts with others in the community. His evenings were filled with meetings and social events — a young marrieds' barbecue, a youth group planning meeting, the Wednesday night congregational prayer meeting.

At first, both Gabriel and Jessica seemed more at ease with the busyness of their work, and with the lack of conversation between them. But when they were in the same room, Gabriel was uncomfortably aware of his heightened interest in her. He found himself absorbed in physical details he couldn't remember finding attractive in any other woman — wisps of hair that had come loose from her ponytail, or the curve of an eyebrow. When he became self-conscious about looking at her face or eyes, he admired the perfect tapered strength of her hands. There was something radiant about her, he told himself. He knew it was a cliché, but it was the only way he could imagine to describe the way she seemed to fill the room with light.

When he had misgivings about whether he should be spending so much time thinking about her, he tried to turn his thoughts into prayers. But he asked himself why it was so easy to be deeply concerned about Jessica's life while his prayers for Marian, and even for his own son, seemed perfunctory and superficial.

He concluded finally that he was only making the situation worse, that the nagging guilt he felt and the questions he kept asking himself were making him more and more obsessed with her. She's an attractive woman, he said to himself. I'm a man. There's chemistry between us, and there's nothing wrong with that. It's the way we're created, something to be celebrated.

After a week, Jessica stopped him as he was hurrying off to an afternoon appointment with the high school principal.

"Gabriel, wait, please," she said. "I get the feeling that you don't want to talk to me any more."

"I'm sorry, Jessica." He felt his face warming. "I'm not trying to avoid you. It's just that there's so much to do."

She stood directly in front of him, looking first into one of his eyes and then the other.

"We do need to talk," he said, cringing inwardly at the banality of his words. "I haven't forgotten."

She reached up quickly and put her arms around his neck. He stiffened with surprise, then encircled her slight body with his arms. "You're a good friend," she said close to his ear, then released him and stepped back.

When he returned to the church late that afternoon, Jessica's car was still there. "You're working a bit late," he called out as he went directly into his office.

He turned to find that she had followed him. She seemed unusually light-hearted, in a way he hadn't seen in her for weeks.

"I'm on my own tonight," she said, "so there's no rush."

"Your family away?"

"No, but I'm staying out at Carsons'. They asked me to watch their place for a couple of days while they're away at Agribition."

"Are you safe there?"

She looked at him curiously and laughed. "Of course. You city people always think that there's some kind of danger when nobody's around."

He watched her, relieved at her lightness of spirit. "Hey, why don't you come out for supper?" she said suddenly. "I'll cook for you, and then we can watch TV or something. And don't say you have a meeting, because I know you don't."

"I don't know." He realized how intensely he wanted to be with her, away from the church and his role, away from the constant intrusion of people's expectations. But he had an uneasy sense of how this might appear to a parishioner, to someone from the community, to a more experienced pastor. To Marian.

"Sure, come on, do it. Leave your car here and come with me. I'll drive you back into town later. Better than going home to that empty house, right? It'll be fun."

It would be fun, he told himself. And it was the perception he was worried about, not the reality. After all, they spent hours together behind the closed doors of the church without giving it a second thought. Why should this be any different? He just had to make sure no one had any reason to be suspicious — to protect both of them from questions.

"Okay," he said, and felt a rush of excitement and anxiety. "But just for a quick dinner. I can't stay late. I have some reading I have to catch up on at home."

When they left the church, the early winter light was blue and fading. She handed him the keys to her car, and they drove out of town, heading west. He was excited to be alone with her again, and he thought about her touch and the way she had felt in his arms earlier in the day. He wanted the drive to last forever, for the deepening gun metal shadows of dusk to become constant and unchanging.

His fingers began to tremble on the steering wheel. He looked straight ahead, but he could feel her eyes on him, could imagine the half smile that curved her lips.

"What are you thinking about?" she asked.

He glanced at her, and felt his emotions lifted by the eagerness of her smile.

"I'm not thinking," he said. "Maybe just feeling."

"Feeling? That's not like you," she teased. "Feeling what?" She unfastened her seatbelt and turned toward him, leaning back against the passenger door. She lifted one leg up on the seat and drew her foot underneath her, and he watched the denim of her jeans stretch tight across her thighs.

"What a good idea this is," he said. "How good it is to be here. With you."

"Yeah," she said, her voice changed, subdued.

He looked to his left, away from her. They were passing a small clearing where a trailer home sat on concrete block pedestals. The place seemed abandoned. There was a cluster of small outbuildings, run down, one of them with a screened enclosure for chickens. His excitement at being alone with her vanished suddenly. He felt trapped and anxious, unsure of why he was there.

"How much further?" he asked.

She looked at him in silence for a moment, not seeming to have heard. She had caught her lower lip with her teeth, and he found the gesture poignantly fragile.

"I don't know," she said, looking ahead, then to the left and the right. "What direction are we going?"

He laughed. "You're the navigator. You're the one who's been where we're going."

The road had narrowed to the width of one lane. A growth of brittle grass down the centre held a shallow covering of snow. He stopped the car and shut off the motor. With the headlights off, the twin tracks of the trail seemed to glow dimly, grey-green, like the underside of a snake. He felt frustration rising in him, and anger at her mixed with guilt and desire. He imagined having to retrace their route, trying to find a farm where they could ask directions, and the questions that would come. His hands were gripping the top of the steering wheel. He let his head rest against them, and closed his eyes.

"Are you praying?" she asked.

He shook his head without lifting it.

"I am," she said, and then, aloud, "Jesus, help us to find our way."

He let out his breath slowly, impatient.

"Gabriel, look!" she whispered.

He sat up. Less than ten yards away, an elk stood at the edge of the road, its head and front quarters emerging from the bush. The elk stretched its neck toward the car, its nose angled upward. The wide antlers extended back horizontally, almost the length of its body.

She caught his hand, gripping his fingers tightly. The elk pivoted its head slightly from side to side, then snorted and moved quickly across in front of the car, disappearing in a darkening stand of aspen and spruce.

They sat in silence. The space in front of them seemed charged with the elk's passing. Gabriel pictured how the fading light had caught the outlines of its neck and haunches, the movement of muscle under hide as it strode across just a few feet away from them. He thought of Jessica's prayer, felt her hand still gripping his own. He had the sense that what he'd just experienced had to happen, that it was inevitable somehow that he was here. He found himself believing that the elk signified something, that it had been sent — a gift, a blessing — in response to her words.

He started the car and began to drive. She watched the road intently, saying nothing. At the next intersection she directed him to the left on a wider road.

"I think this is it," she said after a few minutes. "We're almost there."

They turned onto a rutted driveway that opened to a yard the size of a ball diamond. The headlights caught a house at the edge of the clearing. Its wooden siding was unpainted and rough. He pulled up in front of the house and shut off the motor; the darkness filled with a silence that seemed to have weight and texture.

"We'd better get in and get supper started," she said, grabbing up her bags.

She reached into a tall milk can on the porch for a key, and opened the door. She stepped in ahead of him, and he found himself lagging a step behind her, keeping some distance between them.

Now the trembling that had begun in his fingers seemed to spread across his upper body. His shoulders and back were caught in a chill spasm. He thought of going back to the car, of leaving her here, of trying to find his way back to town alone.

She turned on a light. They were in a large kitchen. The wooden table in front of him held a mason jar with a branch of hawthorn, its dry leaves curled and its thorns as long and straight as sewing needles.

"Why don't you start a fire in there," Jessica said, gesturing toward the darkness of the adjacent living room. "I'll start supper."

He shivered as he passed her, and she reached out to briskly rub his back. She seemed at home here, he thought, and he felt out of place, like a small boy.

He arranged kindling in the fireplace and lit it. Through the crackling of the fire, he heard a cork pop in the next room.

"Want some wine?" she called out. "This is where I can come to drink without my parents knowing."

She walked in carrying the bottle and two glasses. "I put a frozen lasagne in the oven — it'll take an hour to cook." She knelt beside him in front of the fire, and handed him a glass, her finger-tips brushing his against the chilled surface.

He watched her face as she poured the wine, and felt his ambivalence fade. He was out of reach here, away from the expectations that governed his life and absorbed all of his energy. His friendship with Jessica seemed to create its own world, a dream world, a world where elk appeared when invoked, a world where who he was was enough, more than enough.

He watched her pour her own glass, the light of the fire glinting in the flow of wine. She set down the bottle, and held out her glass to him.

"Here's to good conversation, and a lifetime of friendship."

"I'll drink to that," he replied, his mouth dry. He sipped the wine, then set his glass on the floor while he added wood to the fire. His upper arms trembled again. "It's cool in here," he said, "damp." He noticed the sharp musty odour of the house, like suddenly overturned deadfall.

"Turn your back to the fire."

He did as she said, and felt the heat of the blaze through his shirt. She reached across with her free hand and rubbed his back and upper arms, resting her head briefly against his shoulder. He got up and moved to the couch that faced the fire. He took a long gulp of the wine, feeling a warm numbness at the base of his skull. He tipped the glass back again, emptying it.

"This wine is going straight to my head," he said, holding out his glass to her. She moved toward him on her knees and refilled his glass. Her face was in darkness now, silhouetted by the bright firelight in her hair.

"Your hair is on fire," he said.

She rested her upper arm along his thigh, then laid her face against the crook of her arm. "I used to come here to babysit all the time," she said. "I'd often ask if I could stay overnight — I've always felt safe here."

"Only here?"

"Yeah, maybe. And with you."

He reached out to the light in her hair, lifting a few strands and letting them fall. "There must be someone else you can trust. Someone else you're safe with."

"No. They'd all think I was making something out of nothing. They all know my father. They're all his relatives or his neighbours or the parents of the kids he coaches hockey, or the people he goes to church with."

She raised her head and looked at him. "Who would take me seriously, other than you?" The words caught in her throat, and she reached up to brush impatiently at her eyes. He caught her hand.

"Come here," he said, and drew her toward him. She reached up to him, and he held her against his chest. Her clothing was hot from the fire. He waited for her to pull away. For a moment, he was afraid, and knew he had to stop. But she clung to him, and he was conscious only of his desire to hold her. He put his face in her hair. He felt the coolness of her neck on his cheek, and when he turned to press his mouth against her skin, she made a soft, high sound that was almost a cry.

IN THE MORNING, Gabriel walked the few blocks to the church. He felt relief at being out of the house, and the physical exertion of walking eased the raw pain of his guilt. The November morning was chilly, and that too seemed cleansing.

But as he neared the church, he felt a rising anxiety. His impulse was to keep walking, to leave behind all of the settings that kept him anchored to his life. Perhaps if he kept moving, no one could find him, no one could accuse him.

His usual practice was to sit in a front pew and begin the day by reading a psalm, quietly waiting until God seemed real and present. But where could he begin now? Could he even go on — with ministry, with marriage? He thought of Marian and Emmanuel, and was stunned with the enormity of the wrong he had done to them.

Walter's truck was on the street next to Gabriel's car, which was where he had parked it the afternoon before. Walter got out of the truck, followed Gabriel into his study and took his usual seat.

"I came by to see you last night," he said. "Saw the light in your study."

"I must have forgotten it," Gabriel said. "I was tired, so I walked home and went to bed early." He felt a rush of shame at his deception.

"I guess that would explain why your house was dark too." Walter looked at him closely. "No fun going home to a cold bed."

Gabriel felt light-headed and nauseous; he tried to smile. "No. But it won't be much longer until Marian's home."

"No indeed." Walter took off his cap and began tapping the peak against the arm of the chair, watching the motion intently. He looked up at Gabriel, his jaw set and his eyes hard.

"I'll say this once," he began, his voice low. "You be careful with my daughter." He broke off, his jaw working. "A pretty woman is the devil's favourite trap. That's how he's finished off many a better man than you."

He stared at Gabriel, lips pale and compressed. "Remember, Pastor, even Jesus came to bring a sword."

Gabriel felt the pressure of blood under his collar and in his eyes. His breathing became quick and shallow. Walter watched him, then stood abruptly. Gabriel sat unmoving, listening to Walter's heavy footsteps as he left the church

After Walter was gone, Gabriel phoned Jessica and asked her not to come in for the rest of the week. "I need some space," he said to her. "We both need some space."

She agreed, her voice small and distant. The following Sunday, she wasn't at church. After the service, Gabriel called the elders together to ask if he could have the week and the next weekend off so he could spend time in the city with Marian and Emmanuel, and then return with them for the first Sunday of Advent.

"Is that okay with everyone," Walter asked the group of men, his face impassive, "provided the pastor arranges pulpit supply in his absence?" They agreed without discussion.

Gabriel went home and began to pack. He was eager to leave town, but he knew there was nowhere to hide from his guilt. Any sense of reprieve that would come from leaving Jessica and the church behind for a few days would be overtaken by the suffering of being in Marian's presence. But there was nothing else to be done. If anything of his life were to continue — marriage, parenting, vocation, faith — he had to keep taking one blind step after another.

Throughout the week that followed, Gabriel avoided conversation by playing with Emmanuel whenever he was awake, and by going shopping with Marian. At night, he stayed up late to read. She was happy here, he thought, in her parents' house.

After he and Marian returned from the city, on the Monday of the first week of Advent, Jessica came into his office and sat down.

"I've locked the front door," she said, "so we won't be interrupted by anyone." She was pale. "Tell me what you want me to do."

He looked at her for a long moment. "I want you to get away from here," he said finally. "Away from this town, away from this church, away from me — and away from your father."

"He won't let me."

"I think he will. Start school somewhere, anywhere. Just make the break."

She was silent for a few minutes. "Do you love me?"

Despite his desolation, he felt a moment of joy, like a glimpse of pale sunlight falling across a distant field.

"The truth is I do," he said weakly. "There's no point in denying it."

They looked at each other without speaking. Through his guilt and turmoil, he had a curious sense of being safe with her. He had risked everything, and because of that he felt closer to her than he might ever be with anyone else. She had seen him at his worst, with all of his well-practised roles stripped away, and she still cared for him.

"I wish," he said, and stopped.

"What do you wish?"

"I don't know. I don't know what to wish for."

Pain shone out suddenly from her eyes. "You wish that I was gone."

"No, Jessica. That's not what I wish for. But I think it might be the best we can do. Nothing more can happen between us. I love you. But I love my son. I love Marian. As long as she'll have me, I'm going to stay."

"Did you tell her?"

He shook his head. "I think I need to, but I don't know when, or how."

She began to wipe tears from her face. He watched her, desolate. Could she ever be comforted, he asked himself. Could he ever be forgiven?

IN THE WEEKS that followed, he carried out his responsibilities mechanically. He told himself that Christmas was like a theatrical production; he knew what the performance required, both at church and with family, and he was determined go through with it. He and Jessica arranged their work schedules so that they were never alone in the church at the same time.

Late on New Year's Eve, when he and Marian were home in bed after a snowmobile party with the congregation, he told her that he had something to say.

"I need to try to put the old year behind me," he began. The words seemed empty and foolish. They lay side by side with the lamp on, not touching. He told her all that had happened, in a tone that sounded flat and lifeless in his own ears.

"You're a coward, Gabriel," she said coldly when he had finished. "That's your problem. It was easier for you to sleep with her than to muster up the courage to do the right thing. You failed that girl as much as you failed me or Emmanuel or anyone else."

They were silent for a long time.

"What are we going to do now?" she asked.

"I don't think I can stay here," he said. "I think we should move back to the city and try to make a new start. You'll be close to your parents. They'd love to see more of Emmanuel."

For the first time, she turned to watch his face as he spoke. "Do you want me to stay with them? Is that what you're saying?"

"No, Marian. If you wanted to leave me, I would understand. But I don't want that. You and Emmanuel are all I have left."

He heard what was unsaid in his words, that if she left he'd have neither Jessica nor her, and he knew that she heard it too. But he felt defenceless, no longer able to choose his words in ways that protected him.

THE NEXT DAY, New Year's, he wrote his letter of resignation, effective at the end of January. That same day, Jessica moved to Lethbridge to start university.

In the weeks that followed, he and Walter said only what was necessary to each other. Walter's aggressiveness seemed to fade. Perhaps, Gabriel thought, they both knew, or guessed, too much about the other.

On Gabriel's last Sunday, Walter was the last to leave. He approached Gabriel and stood awkwardly for a moment. Out of habit, Gabriel began to extend his hand, then withdrew it.

Walter's eyes crossed Gabriel's face, then he looked away. "I'm not the man you think I am." His voice seemed tentative. "Remember that."

Walter opened the door and walked away, leaving it open behind him.

Gabriel watched him go. He thought about Walter's words. Perhaps he was not the man Walter thought he was either. Perhaps there were possibilities for him beyond Walter's judgement, and beyond his own. He stepped out through the open door of the church for the last time and closed it behind him.

Reasons

THAT THURSDAY, THE EARLY MORNING SKY WAS MARKED WITH the northward flight of geese. Tools slung over his shoulder, Stephen stopped to watch them — there was lots of time to make the four blocks from his basement suite to the bus stop. It was a small flock, less than n hundred, and they were low enough that he could hear the hiss of air against their wings. The formation began to falter, and the geese circled back to the right. Small groups of two or three broke off from the flock.

He laughed quietly to himself. He wasn't the only one who felt out of place — even the geese seemed lost in the city. Hungry for open space, he watched them a moment longer. He glanced at his watch and resumed walking. His brief glimpse of the geese made him feel wide awake and more alive, and his step seemed lighter on the pitted surface of the sidewalk.

He took a window seat on the bus, and watched the passing houses. After a couple of months in the city, it still seemed remarkable to him that they were so close together. In places, their eaves almost touched. Convenience stores and strip malls began to appear amongst the residences, and then apartment buildings and businesses began to dominate his view. As they passed a large shopping mall, he noticed a single car parked on the vast expanse of empty pavement, motor running. A man got out of the driver's seat and stretched. Who was he, Stephen wondered, and what was he doing in such an unlikely place at this time of the morning?

There were few passengers on the bus at first, but it filled gradually. The subdued roar of the diesel motor was punctuated with the hiss of brakes and the clatter of coins. Many of the passengers greeted the driver as if he were a friend, and some sat close to him at the front to resume conversations that never seemed to reach any conclusion. One of the regular passengers greeted Stephen, and he nodded in response. But he turned back to the window without speaking. Perhaps he seemed unfriendly, but he found it hard to know where to begin. At home, everyone knew something about you, so conversation seemed easier.

At seven-fifteen, he got off at the last stop before the route turned back toward the centre of the city. He began to walk again, this time on the new pavement of a recently developed subdivision. The black surface of the street was lightly coated with frost, and it reminded him of the low spots in the summerfallow fields back home, of how the alkali lay white on the dark soil.

He was always the first of the framing crew to arrive in the morning. The job site was muddy and cluttered. It was hard for him to imagine that this would be someone's neighbourhood in just a few months, with the playgrounds that were nothing more than drawings now filled with noisy children. The two-storey townhouse units they were constructing were scattered at seemingly random angles across the site. In contrast to the bare clay underfoot, the new lumber of the buildings glowed a clean golden colour in the morning light.

He'd come to the city from the family farm in January. Despite occasional employment at the curling rink in town, he'd been restless after a couple of months of the more relaxed work routines that followed harvest. He'd been reluctant to move to the city, but he liked the work. At nineteen, he had little job experience other than the farm, but he was hardworking and good with a hammer, and he had caught on quickly.

He buckled on his toolbelt, settling the heavy leather pouches against his narrow hips. He checked for his tape measure and chalkline, then sharpened his flat red and black carpenter's pencil with a few strokes of his knife. He thought back to where he had left off work the day before. He had been measuring and marking out the second floor interior walls of a building on the far side of the job site. To the casual observer, every townhouse was identical, but to Stephen's meticulous eye, no two were ever exactly alike.

"That's the luxury unit I'm working on," he'd commented, straight-faced, one day at coffee. "An extra inch and a half in the living room." The others looked at each other, not knowing what to make of his remark. No one laughed.

The foreman, Tony, pulled up in his truck just before eight, and the rest of the crew arrived soon after. Stephen went to help unload the compressors, air-powered nail drivers, power saws and heavy black coils of extension cords.

"Wayne's coming back today," Tony announced, not seeming to address anyone in particular. Three or four men close to the truck were suddenly attentive.

"You're taking Wayne back?" Harry asked, incredulous. "Tony, what the hell you want with him?"

"So he screwed up," Tony replied. "He needs a break — and you know as well as I do how hard it is to find someone with experience these days."

"Yeah, right, Tony," Harry said, his voice filled with disgust. "That and he's your cousin's ex-brother-in-law or some such thing. Just don't put him anywhere around me."

"Shut up, Harry. You'll do what I say like everybody else."

Tony turned back to the truck. "I'm putting him in Unit Six where Stephen is — that way he can work more or less on his own. He can frame those walls you're laying out, Stephen. He'll have to do it by hand. We don't have enough power nailers to go around."

"Good luck, kid," Harry muttered. "Stay as far away from the guy as you can."

Stephen wondered what had happened between Harry and the new man in the past. Whatever it was, it probably wasn't as serious as he made it sound. Harry was one of the vocal ones on the crew, and Stephen thought he had a tendency to exaggerate.

Wayne arrived just before nine, after the rest of the crew had settled into the rhythm of their work. Stephen heard his heavy steps as he entered the building at ground level, and the rasp of his breathing as he pulled himself up the ladder to the second floor. Stephen smelled a cigarette, then watched Wayne's thick neck and broad back appear through the stairwell opening. He stepped off the ladder with a grunt, and stood with his back to Stephen, one hand resting on the temporary wooden railing nailed up around the opening. He took a drag on his cigarette, flicked the butt away, then stepped away from the stairwell. He was heavy and long-limbed, with the careful, unwasted movements of the overweight. He turned and surveyed Stephen, his face expressionless and reddened with exertion.

"Tony says you can start at the far end," Stephen said. "There's studs and headers and cripples already in each unit." He hesitated, unsure of how much to offer. "I'm Stephen. Let me know if you have any problems."

Wayne shifted on his feet and let out his breath through his nose. He looked Stephen over, disdain showing on his wide face. "Problems," he snorted. "I've forgotten more about framing than you'll ever know, you skinny little fuck. If I have any problems, it'll be because you buggered up, *Stephen*."

Stephen shrugged and turned to go back to his work. "Hey," Wayne shouted, not moving, "I'm not finished talking to you. Where the hell's the spikes?"

"They're right at the top of the ladder," Stephen replied evenly. But he could feel his heartbeat, quick and insistent against his ribs. "You walked right past them."

Stephen went back to work, and soon heard the steady sound of Wayne's hammer. Even at the distance between them, he could make out the heavy wheeze of Wayne's breathing. At coffee time, Wayne dropped his tools first. When Stephen came into the building they used for a lunch room, Wayne was already sitting on the floor, his back against a half sheet of plywood he had leaned up against the wall.

"It's not the way I would have done it," he was saying to Tony as Stephen came in. "But what can you expect? Like you say, he's just a kid fresh off the farm. Probably still got shit on his boots."

Wayne looked at Stephen. "I was just telling Tony about the fucked-up way you laid out those walls."

Stephen felt his face muscles tighten with anger. But he turned away. He sat down at the edge of the group farthest away from Wayne and the conversation moved on around him.

After coffee, Tony called him over. "How's Wayne working out?"

Stephen shrugged and looked away. "I don't know. I haven't checked."

"Might not hurt to have a look," Tony said, then added, "I can come and do it if you like."

"It's all right," Stephen said, "I'm going that way."

"Thanks," Tony said. "Don't let the guy get to you. He's a certified asshole — but every asshole's got his reasons."

"I suppose," Stephen said. He turned away abruptly and walked back to the building where he had been working. He pushed his way through the open-studded walls to where Wayne stood strapping on his toolbelt.

"Tony wanted me to see how it's going," Stephen said, inspecting Wayne's work quickly. In places, the grey nail heads protruded slightly from the surface of the wood. He reached for his hammer and drove them home.

Wayne watched him. "What do you think you're doing with my walls?"

"Finishing them," Stephen replied, not looking up.

"Listen," Wayne said slowly, raising a slab of an arm to point at him. "If I finish something, it's finished. Just ask the last fucker who tried to get me fired."

"Nobody's trying to get you fired." Stephen felt his chest tighten. He wanted to go back to his own work with as little trouble as possible, but the shoddiness of Wayne's work irritated him. He banged one last nail head tightly into the soft spruce lumber.

He could feel Wayne watching him as he turned away. He walked with a careful casualness, but he felt a tremor in his legs. He resumed his work quickly, hoping to open up more distance between himself and Wayne.

At lunch time, Wayne settled himself heavily in the centre of the scattered group of workers and flopped open a large metal lunchbox. He ate in huge bites, and talked affably while he ate, pulling some of the newer members of the crew into the conversation. They compared the construction companies they'd worked for, the bars they drank in, the stupidest foremen they'd known. Wayne's circle of attention grew, and he addressed four or five of them by name. He never looked in Stephen's direction, except once.

"Gotta hate them brown-nosers," he pronounced as the conclusion to one of his stories. Then he looked at Stephen pointedly, and his face became wooden, his eyes hard.

Stephen looked away and didn't reply. There was a tight, crawling sensation in his stomach. All he wanted was to be anonymous, to do his work and mind his own business. For an instant, he imagined his workboot driving into Wayne's face, Wayne's skull smashing back into the wall behind him. But he pushed the thought away, and forced the clenched muscles of his arms and hands to relax.

After lunch, Stephen finished marking out the interior walls. He asked Tony what to do next, hoping to move to another part of the job site.

"I don't know if I want to leave Wayne entirely on his own," Tony said. "I don't trust him enough to put him with the new guys, and he's burnt his bridges with everybody else. Why don't you start framing where you just finished laying out, and work back towards him. If he gives you any problems, let me know."

Stephen went back to work reluctantly, but he warmed to the vigorous rhythm of his hammer. He stopped to pull off his jacket, and glanced toward where Wayne was working. Wayne looked up.

"What are you staring at?" he snarled across the forty feet between them. "Got nothing better to do than check up on everybody else's work? Why don't you come over here and have a closer look."

Stephen didn't reply. The spring sunlight shone down on the unroofed building where they worked, and the sky was clear. He found himself thinking of what it had been like at his high school on afternoons like this — he remembered the lightness that he felt when he walked out the door at the end of the day for the ride home on the bus, the green of the first growth in the ditches beside the road. The feeling seemed distant now, and he wondered if it was a part of life that was gone for good.

At afternoon coffee, the crew seemed tired and was mostly silent. Stephen filled his cup from his thermos and felt the steam passing over his face. Across from him, Wayne turned a nail between his fingers, then flipped it through an empty window opening. He reached for another, and Stephen looked away. The nail bounced off the sleeve of Stephen's shirt and splashed into his cup.

"Bingo," Wayne said, and there was a short laugh from someone else. "Right on the money."

Stephen said nothing. He fished the nail out of the hot coffee and tossed it aside. He could feel Wayne looking at him, turning another nail over in his hand, but he kept his eyes down.

The nail hit the wall behind Stephen and bounced off. Stephen flinched but didn't look up.

"Should get me a power nailer," Wayne said. "Then we could really do something."

The third nail hit just above his right eye. Stephen felt the sting of the sharp edge of the nailhead against his skin, and the wet heat of spilled coffee on his thigh. He pushed himself to his feet.

Harry slammed his thermos onto the plywood floor. "Why don't you leave the kid alone?"

The sound of Harry's voice seemed to break the urgency of Stephen's anger, and he sat down again, feeling his control return. "Don't worry about it, Harry," he said, his eyes on Wayne. "That fat ass is better at throwing nails than he is at driving them."

Wayne's face contorted. He pulled himself to his feet, fists clenched, and started toward Stephen. Tony scrambled up and moved between them.

"Sit down, Wayne," Tony yelled. "Just sit down. If you so much as throw one punch — hell, if you give me fucking indigestion I'll have you off this crew and back where you came from."

For a moment the room was still. Wayne stood facing Tony, his face frozen and his fist half raised. Then he took a step backward, smiled broadly and lowered his arm.

"Tony, don't get your dick in a knot. I wasn't going to do anything. I was just having some fun with the kid."

Stephen heard someone exhale loudly. Harry tossed the last of his coffee on the floor and fastened the cup to his thermos with a few quick turns.

"Let's get back to work," Tony said, his voice flat. Stephen got up and buckled on his toolbelt. He was light-headed, as if he'd been awakened suddenly, and when he touched a finger to the scratch on his forehead, it came away with a spot of blood on it.

Tony approached him. "I'm putting you somewhere else for the rest of the day," he said. "You can clean all the scrap out of Unit One — haul it over to the dumpster."

It was a way out, Stephen knew. But temporary.

"What's the point, Tony? He's going to be back tomorrow. One way or another, I'm going to have to deal with him. Right?"

Tony looked away. "He can be an ugly bastard." He paused and looked back at Stephen. "Any sign of trouble, get the hell away from him, you hear? The last time Wayne was on the crew he had something going with one of the guys — beat the shit out of him one night after they'd been drinking. Wayne's just out on parole now."

"So why'd you take him back?"

Tony shrugged. "Like I said, every asshole's got his reasons."

Wayne was stooped over, hammering steadily, when Stephen returned to his work. The sun was lower, and he felt a chill pass over him. He pulled on his jacket and turned his back toward Wayne.

Stephen's throat was dry, and he felt a twinge of nausea. He was afraid, he knew, and his fear made him angrier. A sudden rush of hatred rose in him like vomit. He could picture Wayne without looking, the thick neck and flat, immobile face. He swung his hammer viciously, and the nail he was driving twisted to one side.

He swore softly and reached for another nail. He was aware of the silence behind him, then heard the heavy rasp of Wayne's breathing coming closer, and his soft grunt as he pushed himself through the cage-like framing of the walls that separated them.

Stephen straightened and watched him approach. He felt a cold stillness come over him — whatever was going to happen, he wanted it over now. Wayne came to the last stud wall that stood between them and kicked out suddenly, splintering a two-by-four loose from the bottom plate. He grabbed it and pulled it free, and stepped through the opening, his movements slow and deliberate.

"Why don't you yell for Tony?" he said in a low voice. "Tell him you're about to have an industrial accident."

He lunged toward Stephen, the splintered end of the stud spearing toward his chest. Stephen twisted to one side. The wood caught him high on the arm. He felt his jacket tear, then the skin beneath it. His hammer fell from his hand. Wayne stumbled, dropped the board, and Stephen scrambled back away from him.

A stud lay between them, on edge. Stephen kicked it, and the end jammed into Wayne's ankle. He bellowed, and Stephen went for him, aiming his fist at Wayne's face. Wayne feinted to the side, and Stephen felt his knuckles scrape across his cheek. Wayne clutched at him, grabbed his arm and threw him heavily against the wall.

Before he could get up, Wayne was on him, his hammer drawn back. Stephen flattened himself as Wayne swung. The hammer hit the wall behind him, and he rolled to the side and regained his feet. Wayne stood sneering, legs spaced widely.

"Next time I'm gonna break your skull, farmboy," he panted.

He would do it, Stephen realized with a rush of dread. Wayne would stop at nothing. Stephen was cornered. His arm was throbbing. He heard a distant laugh from somewhere on the job site, and considered calling for help. But there wasn't time for anyone to reach him now. The sunlight was slanting low across the floor; every grain of sawdust seemed to glow. He saw the empty stairwell behind Wayne. He pushed himself off the wall, saw Wayne's hammer come up. Stephen jumped, feet first, and kicked his boots into Wayne's gut. Wayne stumbled backward, arms flailing, and hit the makeshift railing. It came loose with a screech of nails, and he went over, screaming as he fell, his voice high and hoarse.

Stephen got up from where he'd fallen and looked down the stairwell. He could see Wayne's sprawled shape on the unfinished dirt floor of the basement twenty feet below him, face up, one leg twisted strangely to the side. Wayne moaned, but he didn't move. Stephen picked up his hammer, and climbed down the ladder slowly. He stepped out of the building, and Tony ran toward him, breathing hard.

"What's going on? I heard somebody yell."

"He fell down the stairwell," Stephen said.

"How'd it happen?" The foreman was staring at the bloody tear on Stephen's arm.

Stephen felt tired, too tired to answer. "It happened, Tony, things happen. You better call an ambulance."

Tony seemed fixed in place for a moment. Then he turned and ran toward the truck. Stephen's legs shook, and he went to lean against the building, then sat on the ground, resting his head back against the plywood wall. He heard a moan from the basement and a muttered word he couldn't make out, then silence. He closed his eyes. He felt no remorse, only hatred. If it had been forty feet down, a hundred feet, he would have done the same. Somewhere above him, he heard a flock of geese cross the sky. The air whistled through their wings, and their cries seemed urgent as they receded into the distance. He didn't look up.

THE AMBULANCE ARRIVED fifteen minutes later. They lowered a stretcher into the basement, strapped Wayne onto it, then six of the men hoisted the stretcher out with ropes. Wayne's face was the colour of dry cement. His eyelids fluttered open, but his eyes were unfocused. There was blood around his mouth and nose, and dark streaks of it had dried on his jacket.

"When I'm finished at the hospital, I sure could use a beer," Tony said as the ambulance left. "Anybody want to meet me for a beer?"

Several of the crew agreed. Harry looked at Stephen.

"There's one or two of us waiting in line to buy you a beer, kid," Harry said. "It'll be just the ticket for that arm. What do you say?"

"Sure," Stephen told him. "Can I catch a ride?"

The men picked up their tools and turned to go. The clouds were golden, scattered in the cold blue of the evening sky. Stephen felt a wave of exhaustion. His legs were sluggish, and the mud underfoot dragged at his boots as he followed Harry toward his truck.

A Man's Gotta Do

IT'S A SUNNY SUNDAY MORNING IN APRIL. I'M SITTING ON THE roof, communing with the treetops. In front of me, there's a flat cardboard box with a skylight in it. On one side, I've got my chainsaw, and on the other, a six-pack. Actually, a four-pack now — I've had two beers, and I feel good. I feel ready.

I find the guide holes I drilled through from the attic. I measure out a rectangle, and score the lines into the asphalt shingles — two rafters wide, about five feet long. I take a knife and start cutting along the line through the shingles, and I peel them back, exposing the clean plywood underneath.

When I'm finished with the shingles, I pick up the saw and hold it in my left hand. I pull the starter cord with my right hand, and it barks and makes that one-of-a-kind chainsaw rattle-buzz-roar into the spring morning. I rev it, think about the neighbours in their beds, and I grin.

I nudge the tip of the saw against the roof, just inside the cut edge of the shingles, and it kind of floats there for a second before it starts to catch. I ease the saw through the plywood and slide the blade carefully just along the side of a rafter. In my framing crew days they called me Doctor Chainsaw — I made those hard-to-reach cuts as straight and clean as most guys could with a power saw, and without the hassle of extension cords.

I still have the touch. I can feel it in my palms, in my fingertips.

"Doctahh Chainsaw," I say out loud, and I like the way the name plays on my tongue.

I make four cuts, one for each side of the rectangle where the skylight will go. The saw spits back plywood splinters, and the roof is slippery with sawdust. I switch off the saw. A little cloud of hot black exhaust drifts away like incense on the spring breeze.

THE FIRST TIME she comes in, Jen notices the floor. She crouches down and runs her hand over it. Unusual, I think, under the circumstances.

We met earlier that night, at a party at the house of some friends. Everybody else seems to be married or with someone — so I get close to a bottle of wine. Dizzy and sad sort of, I'm keeping the couch warm, feeling distant from the legs dancing around me and the always-surprised tone of the conversations. Suddenly she sits down close to me, and leans back, out of breath.

"I like a tall man," she says, and gives me a sideways look.

It takes a beat or two to realize she's talking about me. I grin and stick out my hand.

"Name's Warren. The tall man with the thinning hair."

She laughs and takes my hand. I laugh too.

It's her legs that appeal to me first — long, with that nice lean look just above the knees, but not so skinny as to diminish the delights that thighs were meant to give. She's wearing a pleated skirt, and it rides up high. As we talk, I steal glances.

Finally, I notice that she's beautiful, entirely beautiful. Most men have that cased right off the top, but not me. Beauty has a mind of its own with me — reveals itself in its own good time.

In mid-sentence, I falter and forget the point I'm trying to make about Neil Young vis-à-vis, say, Bob Dylan. She's looking at me, her dark eyes distant, nose strong and straight. She's a bit amused, bemused maybe. Her mouth is open a little, like she's about to say something — she can taste the words. And they taste so good she'll keep them to herself.

Then the mouth grins, and what it really says is, "Quit staring and ask me to dance." It's a slow, sappy song, and when she comes into my arms, she feels like all I've ever wanted.

IT'S THE BEGINNINGS of things that I live for. The hot, heady rush of desire and discovery early in a relationship — like pushing off blindfolded for a fast downhill run. Or a brilliant idea, as if it came on a stone tablet from the Man Himself, for getting more space out of a shoebox-size closet. The title for the great Canadian novel, or the first glimpse of bare wood under the sharp blade of the paint scraper.

I can believe in perfection then — right here, at my fingertips. And I reach for it, thinking maybe this time it will last.

THE NIGHT OF THE PARTY, the night we met, we're in her Corolla in front of my house. We're kissing like two kids, exploring each other's mouths with our tongues, crazy for the touch of skin under clothing. I'm twisted toward her, the hand brake digging into my leg. Her knees are up high against the underside of the steering wheel, and I slide my hand over a knee, along that thigh, under that skirt.

She pulls away and grabs my hand. "Wait," she says. "This is silly."

I move back into my seat, steeling myself for disappointment.

"You have a bed in that house?" she says. "With a bit more room than this?"

We take a long time at the door. I'm reaching in all my pockets to try to find the key, and she's reaching in all my pockets, double-checking. Finally, I get the key in the lock, and I push her through in front of me, my face in her hair, my arms around her waist.

“What a great colour,” she says when she sees the entrance of my house. It’s blue, intense, like Lake Louise mixed with sky. She stops to look at it and smiles, and then she notices the oak floor, and she’s down on her knees running her hands over the finish.

She’s unusual, but I like it.

“Come see what I’ve done with the bedroom,” I say. ‘The bed’s up in a loft, sort of, with a desk underneath.”

She gets up while I’m talking and gives me a long look, pleased and curious all at the same time. “Can’t resist a man with a loft,” she says, and kisses me. She hooks her fingers in my belt and pulls me closer. “Especially with a desk underneath.”

Later, we’re lying side by side. Her hand is in my hair, and I move my face across her breasts, her nipples brushing my eyelids. Her leg is up over my side, and with my hand I follow the line of her leg, all the way from her toes to her ankle, her calf, knee, thigh, over her buttock — until my fingers find the wet, hot place our bodies join.

She pushes against me, rolls her weight on top of me. As she starts to sit up, I put my hands on her breasts. She arches her back suddenly, hits her head hard on the ceiling, and I feel the impact through my crotch. She collapses down against me then, moaning and laughing, and I start to laugh too, uncontrollably.

“Maybe this loft just wasn’t meant for me,” she says into my neck.

I’m already thinking, it was only meant for you.

JEN’S NOT ONLY BEAUTIFUL, she’s smart.

I mean, I’m smart too, in a B.A. Honours kind of way. But I’ve got a mind that wanders, explores, that never really goes in one direction for long. Like a dog with a good nose and a full belly who says to himself, “Hmm, there’s an interesting scent. Let’s just have a sniff. No, wait! Here’s a different one — we’ll have a go at that! But, come to think of it, I was onto a bit of a trail over here. . . .”

You get the picture. Like the beginning of an Altman movie.

But Jen's got a hungry dog kind of mind that knows what trail's important and where it's going.

Like the first of our conversations when she's asking what I want in life, and I think I'm telling her, but she doesn't seem to be taking to the answer.

"So, Warren," she says. "You want work to do that doesn't occupy too much of your time. When you step out of your home office you want a woman to come home to. You want a couple of renovation projects on the go and a few more to fantasize about. A movie and some great tunes now and then. When you're thirsty a cold beer and inane conversation with your buddies. And that's it? You do that for sixty years, and then you kick off?"

That's when I do the bit about loving the journey, not the destination.

And she looks at me straight and cool and hard and says, "Warren, going in circles does not constitute a journey."

Just like that.

See what I mean? She's smart.

JEN MOVES IN — it happens like this:

We're doing coffee after a movie one night, a couple of months after we start seeing each other. She's got a nice two-level townhouse, compact, but her rent's going up and she's not happy. She's got every penny accounted for. By an accountant, no less.

I say, "You could move in with me."

She says, "You mean it?"

I say, "Yeah. It'd be great. If you want to."

She says, "But I'd never get to be on top."

I say, "The ceiling's not that low above the dining room table."

So the next Saturday, she's out front. I go to the door, deliriously happy. All I see is her car.

"Could you give me a hand?" she says, dampening my impulse to carry her over the threshold.

"Sure — but where's the truck?"

A Corolla's not that big.

"No truck," she says. "I put my bed and couch and table and chairs into storage. The rest is in the car."

"Wow!" I manage, always the master of the clever riposte.

"I have a streamlined life," she says. "Lean and mean. No baggage."

An hour later, after everything's in and hung and shelved, we go back for the baggage.

"I have some," she confesses over a cappuccino I whip up as a welcome.

I know she's been married, but now she talks about it. She was young, he was handsome. She was insecure, he knew exactly what he wanted. She was at home, learning to be a housewife. He was out doing deals, and at night he wanted a good square meal, a listening ear, and hot sex.

Now I'm the one doing the listening. I'm a good listener.

When she's finished she says, "How about you, Warren? Let's hear your deep and dirty secrets."

"What do you mean?" I say.

"Any baggage — divorce, illegitimate children, abuse given or received, criminal record? That sort of thing."

"No — innocent on all counts."

"Come on," she says. "At least a couple of seriously dysfunctional long-term relationships."

"How long a term did you have in mind?"

"Let's say three years. Half as long as my marriage."

"No," I say. "Would you settle for three months?"

She's quiet for a split second, and then she laughs.

MORNINGS, I LIE IN BED and watch her. With my eyes, I trace the lines of her face, as if I were drawing them. I follow the delicate arc of an eyebrow from the outside toward the centre, feel something like acceleration in the way the curve tightens, sweeps into the perfect straight line of her nose. The bow of her upper lip, pensive in sleep. Tangled hair.

I wonder where the beauty comes from, and why it disappears if you look too closely. The face separates into hemispheres, and I divide her face in my mind, drawing the lines, breaking the lines into segments, stepping out the proportions like a draftsman.

Pretty draws you in, I think, but beauty holds you away.

Making love by candlelight, I stop to look at her, just to look. She reaches for me, impatient, and I brush my fingertips along the flawless skin on the inside of her arm. I feel distant, sad — as if her beauty is promising something I'll never attain. She senses my ambivalence, and she's frustrated, angry. I blow out the candle, and we turn our backs to each other, chilled with sweat, nerves on edge, sleepless.

JEN WORKS six days a week and lots of evenings, managing a clothing store. When she comes home she's tired, but she likes to talk about the store, the things she'd do differently and better if she owned it, if she were really in charge.

I'm doing freelance editing out of my bedroom-slash-office — right now local histories and a couple of newsletters for non-profits. Most days I call it quits at three-thirty or four, and I start supper, or get in a little extra time on one of my never-ending renovation projects.

One winter evening, a couple months after she moved in, we've just finished my pasta-chicken salad. The dishes are in the dishwasher that I finally got hooked up, and we're kicked back with a glass of wine.

"You're too good to me, Warren," she says. "All I have to do is go to work and do my laundry. I tell my friends at the store, and they're green with envy."

"Too bad," I say. "Never developed a taste for green women."

She laughs.

I've had something on my mind, sense an opening.

"Jen, I've been thinking," I start. "Maybe I should cut back a bit."

She seems suspicious. "How does a freelance editor cut back?"

"I'd drop a newsletter or two," I say. "One of my contracts is coming up now. It'd give us more time — it'd give me more time around the house."

"All you are now is around the house," she says. "You get out of bed, you're in the office."

"I'd have time to get some projects finished up around here," I say. "Like that basement bathroom that's been on the go for five years. And more time to cook and clean."

She looks dubious.

"I don't want any more money from you," I say. "It's just that with your rent and grocery money, I don't need to make as much. So what do you think?"

"A house husband," she says. She's quiet, thoughtful — like she's solving a problem at work. "No," she sounds definite. "I don't think it's a good idea."

End of discussion.

THE PHONE RINGS and it's Len — he's coming to Agribition and he wants my couch. I say sure, and I'm excited about seeing him.

"Len and I go back a ways," I tell Jen. I tell her the whole story. I want them to like each other.

When we were kids, Len moved onto the ranch just outside Medicine Hat where he lives now. My dad ran a trucking company, mostly oilfield work, and we had a few acres with a couple of sheds and offices just down the road from Len's dad's place. One day, the summer we were both fourteen, we need to hire extra help to unload a flatbed of drilling mud, so I go ask Len.

"The bags are small," I say, "but they're heavy as hell."

He's small himself — about five-five and a hundred and twenty pounds. And quiet. When I bring him over, my dad looks skeptical, but he doesn't say anything.

Len soon proves himself. He's tough and determined. You can

see he's surprised at the weight when he picks up the first bag, but then he puts his head down and matches the rest of us, bag for bag. When we're almost done, I crouch down on my heels to hoist a bag off the pallet and I lose my balance. I fall backwards onto the deck of the trailer, the bag of mud across my chest. I'm so worn out I can't move — pinned, completely helpless.

Len looks down at me. "Let me help you get something off your chest," he drawls, and he reaches down for the bag, grinning. After that, we're friends.

"We were inseparable," I tell Jen. "In university our buddies called us the Biggest Hippie and the Littlest Hippie. We were like Mutt and Jeff, Simon and Garfunkel."

Len arrives the next afternoon, and we're drinking beer in front of the TV when Jen comes home from work.

"Who's your short friend?" Jen says, as if she doesn't know. Len's not much bigger at thirty-five than he was at fourteen.

Before I can apologize for Jen, he's on his feet, nodding and grinning, shaking her hand and saying, "You didn't tell me she was so beautiful," or some such thing.

By the time I get supper on the table, they're talking business. Len's telling her how he paid for his first truck, and about the thoroughbreds he's raising.

"Some day," he says, "I'd like to be the major Western Canadian breeder."

"A little dream all the boys had once," I say, but neither one of them notices.

I think it's a good line, so I laugh.

I DON'T TELL JEN, but I drop one newsletter, and then another. Her rent makes up for one of them, her grocery money just about covers the other.

In my spare time, I get the basement bathroom done and drywall the garage. I'm starting some shelving in the rec room downstairs when she starts asking questions.

It's none of her concern, but I tell her anyway.

She doesn't say anything. But she's pissed off. Really pissed off.

IN JANUARY, Len comes to town for a horse show. When he arrives, he's dressed for it too — he's looking like a slightly scaled-down version of the Marlboro man. Jen's really happy to see him. At night, he wants us both to go to the show with him, but I've got a coat of paint I can't wait to get at so Jen goes with him.

Next evening at the supper table, they're talking business again. "An up-market western clothing store would make a killing in the Hat," Len says, and Jen's really listening. "Here would be okay too, but there's a better market in Alberta. You'd get customers from Brooks to Swift Current to Oyen and down to Havre."

"I don't think I'm ready for my own store," Jen says. "I don't have the money. And I don't know anything about western wear."

"You'd learn fast," Len says. "And the money's there for the person with the right idea."

What a capitalist you've turned out to be, I'm thinking. What happened to the Littlest Hippie?

Toward the end of the horse show, Jen comes home late for supper and Len's with her. "Look what I've got, Warren," she says.

She's got boots.

Len sidles up to me. "One look at those legs, Warren, and I knew she had to have boots. What do you say?"

I could say, you two are late for supper and why didn't you call, but I look at those long legs in tight jeans and boots, and I'm breathless. And then she takes a new felt hat out of a bag and puts it on, and I stare like a thirteen-year-old who's just got his hormones.

Len's leaving after supper, so I get them to sit on the couch with the new duds. Jen snuggles up to him and flips her arm over his shoulders. She's got a leg up so I can catch her boot in the viewfinder, and I say they look good together.

"Lenny and Jenny," I say. "Just like on that album about the raincoat. The famous one."

They laugh. But right after I say their names together, while they're looking at me through the camera, an odd expression flits across both their faces, like they thought I could read their minds.

After Len's gone, I ask how much she paid for the boots.

"Len paid for everything," she says. "He insisted — and he certainly can afford it."

My mind isn't on Len's money. I find the Famous Blue Raincoat album and put it on, thinking Lenny's songs and Jenny's voice will set the mood for both of us. But Jen seems listless and distracted. She wants sex, but she wants it to be over quick so she can get to sleep.

TWO WEEKS LATER, Len's back.

"I'm going to get a hotel room this time," he says to me, and I can't change his mind. "Three's a bit crowded."

When we're all together, almost every conversation is about the store Jen wants to open — which is sounding more and more like the store Len wants her to open. She can't let go of the idea, but you can tell she's scared of the risk.

Len's sympathetic with her fears, but he won't back down. "I know what you're feeling, Jen," he says. "I felt the same before I bought my first breeding stock. But in the end, I just had to do it — I felt almost as if it was my destiny."

"A man's gotta do what a man's gotta do," I say, a bit sarcastic.

At that, Jen notices I exist. She's irritated.

"And what do you gotta do, Warren?" she asks.

"I don't gotta do," I reply. "I say a man doesn't gotta do."

"Maybe he does," she says, quieter. "If he's a man, he's gotta do something."

I'm thinking, a man's gotta be what a man's gotta be. But I say nothing.

"THIS HOUSE IS YOU," Jen says.

It's a Saturday morning in February and we've just finished coffee. I'm on my back under the sink, knees up, reaching to try to connect the water supply tubes under a new kitchen faucet. She's standing next to my feet, tapping her nails on the ceramic tile top of the island.

"In fact, Warren," she says, "it's more you than you are yourself."

I lift my head a little and look out at her machine-tanned ankles. They're crossed, her lovely right foot resting tiptoed against the floor.

"You're beautiful," I say, "but you're not making sense."

Suddenly the ankles uncross and she reaches down and gooses me, hard. I start to sit up fast, and I smash my face against the trap under the sink.

"Shit," I moan, and I slump back in pain.

She doesn't sympathize, or even laugh. This is serious, so I crawl out from under the sink, wincing and holding my nose. She's still standing by the island, arms crossed. I stay on the floor and lean back against the cupboard doors, checking for blood as a way to stall for time.

"Talk to me," I say, feeling tired. "What's going on?"

She shakes her head and lets out her breath. Then she turns her back and walks across to the French doors that open onto the deck. I can see the snow piled against the doors, and right now it seems the winter's been too long.

"I'm sick of this place," she says, and I don't know if it's the house or the city or something less tangible. "Warren, what do you want?" She doesn't sound angry anymore.

"I want you." As soon as I say it, I can hear how trite and inadequate it sounds, but it's true. "What do you want, Jen?"

She turns around and looks at me with that sad, faraway look. "I want a man who finishes as well as he starts," she says. "Someone who isn't in a constant state of renovation."

"I thought you liked a tall man," I say.

"I do," she says. "I thought you were a tall man."

WINTER SEEMS TO BREAK about the first week of March, so I drive to Saskatoon to see a client. When I get back to the house, Jen's gone.

"I'm sorry to do it this way," her note says, "but I just couldn't face you. I took most of my stuff. I'll come back for the rest in a few weeks. Maybe we can talk then. I guess you'll know where I am, and who I'm with."

I sit there for an hour, not moving, my coat still on. Finally, I get up, go out to the car and start to drive.

I STOP AT A CAFÉ just off the highway in a small town east of Medicine Hat. It has an old wood-frame screen door, covered in plastic for the winter, with a diagonal metal 7-Up door pull across it. The walls are covered with cheap woodgrain panelling, which looks even worse under the bare fluorescent lights.

The owner is Chinese. A teenaged girl, probably his daughter, sits in a booth closest to the kitchen, bent over school books. She looks like a princess, as serene and unreachable as a scene painted on rice paper. The cracked vinyl upholstery behind makes her seem out of place, exiled.

The door opens, and an older man comes in, unshaven, wearing a sheepskin coat. He doesn't look around, but goes straight to a booth, sits down, and takes off his heavy leather mitts.

Maybe it used to be straightforward, I think. Being a man. You had a career, you made money. You got married, you had children. Then you bought property and went into debt. Maybe you joined a church or the Lion's Club. You provided for your family, and you kept them in line. You kept your feelings simple and you kept them to yourself. You didn't have to think about what it meant to be a man — you just got it with your hormones, like fluoride in water or iodine in salt.

Like an additive.

When did they stop putting it in?

LEN COMES TO THE PORCH soon after I knock. It's late, but he's fully clothed, buttoned and zipped like a husband.

I go dizzy with rage. "You little bastard," I say, and I grab him by the neck, slam him back against the doorpost. He knocks my arms away, puts his shoulder low against me and drives me across the porch into the wall. I'm gasping for breath, and he moves back quick.

"Don't do this, Warren," he says.

I think of the times we stood in this porch. The time we got up at five on a snowy April morning to go rafting. When I brought him home dead drunk from a grad party, and held him upright, waiting for his parents to unlock the door.

Then Jen is there.

"Warren," she says, sounding surprised. She looks at Len, puts her hand on his arm.

"Are you sure?" he asks.

"It'll be okay," she tells him, and he goes in the house, glancing back at me. I'm still trying to catch my breath.

"God, Warren," she says. "You've come all this way."

She turns partly away from me, leans in the doorway. I hear the TV in the next room, and I imagine them sitting together, holding hands, absorbed in the show. Miserable and helpless, I look at her hair, like spun bronze, tarnished and shining against the green of her sweater.

She's beautiful, I think. Entirely beautiful. It's like seeing her for the first time.

"I'm sorry, Warren," she says. "I needed more."

"Are you moving here?" I ask.

She nods. "I'm going to open that store."

"Better market," I say. "That's what this is about."

She looks at me, startled and hurt. "You know that's not true."

"Then what?" I ask.

She's quiet for what seems a long time. "You didn't do anything," she says. "You didn't even try. Len and I were happening right in front of your eyes, and you just let it happen."

"I'm here now," I say.

"Yeah. Too late." She looks at me again. "But it's a start, Warren. Maybe there's hope for you yet."

Then she reaches out, touches my face. I want to hold her in my arms, but I'm coming apart inside so I turn and get out quick. I drive a mile down the road and I stop, blinded. I hold onto the steering wheel as if it's all I have, and I cry, I sob. It feels like a fist ramming down my throat and tearing the life out of me, handful by handful.

Crying's good for you, they say. Especially for men.

But my diaphragm aches for days.

I SHUT OFF THE CHAINSAW, and go to work with hammer and pry bar. In a flash, I get the plywood sheeting off, and I look through the hole in the roof to the attic and the insulation lying between the ceiling joists. Just on the other side of that ceiling is my bedroom and my bed.

I stand looking down through this space, this fresh wound in my house, and I picture the way the light will fall through the skylight, down through a rectangular shaft lined with cedar boards, painted white.

How perfect it could be. How perfect it could be if she were there above me, stretched back naked under a vault of light and space. Moonlight sifts across her skin, our laughter lifts like heat-borne ash toward the sky.

The Darkness Beneath All Things

WILFRED JERKED UPRIGHT, THE SHARP CRACK OF SPLINTERING WOOD in his ears. Blackness pressed in on him, and his eyes were wide open, desperate for light. He surfaced into consciousness, and the room began to take shape, grey and familiar. He was breathing quickly, and his heart drummed against his chest.

My own bedroom, he said to himself.

My four walls. My window. My house.

He heard the wheels of a vehicle thump over the white rocks that lined his driveway, and the clang of tailgate chains against the metal box of a pickup. He knew the truck now — recognized the sound of Jack Simmons's twenty-year-old Chevy. He heard Jack's curses above the revved-up roar of a motor in first gear. More likely than not, Jack was drunk again.

Wilfred swung his feet to the floor and crossed the room. He switched on the bare overhead bulb and stood, motionless, waiting for his pulse to slow. He took several slow, deep breaths, tried to expel the sharp, trembling sensation from his lungs.

"Easy." The syllables rose and fell like a phrase from a chant. It was the word he would use to soothe an anxious cow as he handled her calf.

He pulled coveralls on over his cotton summer underwear, his movements measured. Jack might fall down in the yard, as he had before, or knock over the geraniums in the milk can at the corner of the front porch. But Wilfred did not allow himself to hurry. To do so only stirred things into turmoil around you. If you moved deliberately, thought deliberately, spoke deliberately, the world would fit itself around you with order and grace.

No one had to get excited. No one had to get hurt.

He finished tying his boots, then walked to the kitchen for a look at the clock on top of the fridge. Two-thirty. He took a plaid jacket from the row of brass hooks in the hallway, pulled it on, and went outside.

Jack's truck had stopped close to the east wall of the chicken house, so close that the headlight beams were small yellow circles against the grey horizontal lines of the wood. Wilfred saw the brake lights flash on and off, so Jack was still in the cab. The motor wasn't running though — Jack had likely hit the brakes hard and stalled it.

Wilfred reached in the open window of the truck and shut off the headlights. Jack was hunched over the wheel, and the air in the cab was heavy with alcohol.

"You all right, Jack?"

"Knocked your sign over, Wilf." Jack's voice was thick, but he said every word distinctly. "You had it too close, I'd say. Too close to the driveway."

"Move over, Jack," Wilfred replied. "Move over and I'll drive you home."

"I don't need you to drive me. I got this far. Right, Wilf? I got this far."

Wilfred looked at the sky. It was a clear, warm night, moonless but bright with stars. The air was still and dry. The truck motor ticked as it cooled.

"Morning's coming, Jack," he said. "Won't be long until we'll have to be up and at it." He thought about the field that he'd started to bale, and the knotter on the baler that needed to be repaired before he resumed work.

"It is morning, Wilf," Jack said, as if explaining something to a child. "Gotta get going." He suddenly reached over and pressed the starter button and the truck jerked forward, the bumper banging into the side of the chicken house.

"Oops," Jack chuckled. "Left her in gear."

Wilfred listened to his chickens cackle excitedly, imagined them stirring on the roost, some of them breaking into short, frantic flights. But they'd settle quickly — they had poor memories, even for the most upsetting experiences.

"Let me drive you home, Jack."

"You got any beer?" Jack asked. "I sure could use a cold one, Wilf."

"Sure. I'll get you one from the house. And then I'll drive you home." Wilfred reached into the cab, turned off the ignition, and pocketed the key.

He wiped his boots carefully on the braided baler-twine mat outside the door. There was one bottle of beer on a shelf in the door of the fridge, and he took it out and set it on the counter. Then he replaced it with one from the half-empty case in the bottom of the kitchen cupboards. If you never had more than one cold in the fridge, Wilfred had often said, you were never tempted to drink more than you should.

"Here's the beer," he said to Jack back at the truck, not handing it to him. "Move over now. You can drink it while I drive."

"Be careful with her," Jack said, dragging himself across the seat. "She's pulling to the left on me."

Wilfred waited for Jack to move, then opened the door and gave him the beer. He switched on the interior light and checked the seat for spills before climbing in.

"We'll have you home soon, Jack." Wilfred started the truck and backed slowly away from the chicken house. By the time they had turned out of the driveway onto the gravel road, Jack was eyeing the half-empty bottle against the light from the dash.

"Could you grab the rest of the case, Wilf?" He sounded worried. "You got to have a beer for yourself. I hate to drink alone."

Wilfred smiled briefly. "You've got my last, Jack. You asked for a cold one, and you've got my last."

"Sure, Wilf." Jack took a long drink. "I've always got your last."

WILFRED GAVE HIS ATTENTION to the road and the truck. Through the steering wheel, he could feel a tug to the left, as Jack had warned. Jack had likely hit a curb, Wilfred guessed, after a long night in the bar at the National Hotel, in town fifteen miles distant. And not long ago either, or Jack would have had it fixed by now. The Chevy was from the early fifties, with running boards a foot wide and curved windows around the back corners of the cab, but Jack took care of it like it was new. Wilfred respected that. It was a good reason to trust Jack, despite his drinking.

They were passing his northwest eighty. To the left of the road, Wilfred could see his stand of wheat, blurred by the motion of the truck, but clean and straight. It was a good crop, tall and thick, with well-formed heads and few weeds. It was a field to be proud of, as much for the way it looked as for what it was worth at harvest time, now just a few weeks off.

Jack cranked down his window, and held the empty bottle out into the wind, playing with the sound of the air across its mouth. Then he flipped it back into the box of the truck. It bounced off a wheelwell and skittered across the steel and hardwood deck, but it didn't break.

Wilfred slowed the truck and turned left.

"Halfway home," Jack said.

They lived four miles apart by road, at opposite corners of a four section square of grainfields and pastureland. Jack was agent for the Rolling Plains elevator, the last trace of a tiny hamlet that bore the same name.

"Won't be long until I'm hauling wheat," Wilfred said. "Are you ready for me?"

Jack was silent for a moment.

"This year," he said. "And then it's over."

The Rolling Plains elevator was to be torn down the following summer, and the railway spur removed. Most of the farmers nearby were already trucking their grain to town.

"It's a shame," Wilfred said. "Any plans yet?"

"They'll let me stay in the house as long as I want," Jack said, a hard edge in his voice. Then, more softly, "I've never lived anywhere else. Born in that house, Wilf. Lots of memories."

Wilfred slowed where the railway tracks crossed the road, then turned to the left and followed the sandy track that led past the elevator to the agent's house.

"Remember when you used to come here with your dad and your kid brother, when my old man was the agent?" Jack asked. "You and Adam — what a livewire that kid was. Lots of fun."

"That's a long time ago," Wilfred replied. "Thirty years."

Wilfred stopped the truck in front of the two-storey house and switched off the lights and ignition. He walked around to open Jack's door, and when Jack made no move to get out, he took his arm. Jack swung his feet around to the running board, then braced himself against the open door as he heaved himself up from the seat and stepped to the ground. Wilfred let his hand fall away, and Jack turned toward the sagging veranda that ran the width of the house.

The inside door of the house opened, and Diane appeared in her housecoat and slippers. She pushed open the screen door, stepped out into the light that spilled from the house and came toward them across the veranda. So much about her had changed, but the way her hips and shoulders moved when she walked was instantly familiar to Wilfred. The recognition always came to him as a surprise, as an unexpected shortness of breath, even though this moment had repeated itself every time he'd seen her over the past twenty years.

"Where'd you find him, Wilfred?"

He squinted against the light from the doorway, but her face was in shadow. She watched them approach, then moved aside to let Jack pass. As always now, her voice sounded thin, resigned.

"In my yard," Wilfred told her. The screen door banged shut as Jack went inside. "I don't know why you wait up after all these years."

She glanced at him, her face lit dimly as she half turned toward the house. She looked worn, Wilfred thought. Once so alive and expressive, her face had become a mask.

"You know me," she said. "I'm a worrier. Come in and have some coffee."

She swung the screen door wide and stepped inside, holding it open behind her without looking back. Wilfred crossed the wooden threshold into the kitchen, closing both doors behind him. Jack was heading for the unlit hallway that opened on the opposite side of the room, stepping carefully into the darkness as if walking downhill.

Wilfred sat down beside the kitchen table. Diane filled a kettle and placed it on a burner of the gas stove. With her back to him, she went to the cupboards and took out a jar of instant coffee, a box of sugar cubes, and a mug. She opened a drawer for a spoon, and brought everything across to the table. There was something about the precision of her movements that said to Wilfred that she expected him to be watching her. He wasn't sure if she wanted that and he looked away.

"Just help yourself when the water boils," she said. "I'll get Jack settled, then I'll drive you home."

The kitchen was worn, but meticulously clean. As always, it seemed smaller now than it did in his childhood memories. Wilfred twisted open the instant coffee and carefully levelled a spoonful of the granules.

Steam began rising from the kettle, and Wilfred got up from his chair and crossed the kitchen to the stove. He poured water into his mug, then sat down again and stirred mechanically.

He remembered the wood stove that once stood across the room; as a child he had admired its polished chrome trim. There was little trace of it now — a round tin cover high on one wall where the stovepipe once joined the chimney, and scars on the linoleum from the stove's feet.

The flooring hadn't been changed from the time of his earliest memories of this room, he realized suddenly. Even now, its pattern was startlingly familiar, a pale green background with an intricate weaving of ivy that divided the floor into interlocking squares. There were openings in the ivy in places, and in the corner of each of the squares, a rose, pale and worn.

"Gateways," Wilfred mumbled, and smiled at the memory. "Gateways and rose fields."

He remembered his metal toy truck, with chipped blue paint, red wheels, and rubber tires, and how he steered the truck through the maze of ivy hedges, brighter green then, turning through what he imagined as gateways into perfectly ordered rose fields. Here, while he waited for his father to dump his grain at the elevator, he delivered truckloads of roses around the ivy-hedged countryside of the agent's kitchen floor.

And across from him was the wood stove, its heat welcome but fierce. On the floor at one end of the stove, he pictured Jack, a red-cheeked six-year-old, and beside him, three years younger, Wilfred's brother Adam, with the blackened coal shuttle behind him. Laughing, Jack and Adam pounded the floor with their hands and shouted, "C'mon, Wilfie, bring us a load of roses!"

Wilfred breathed deeply and wiped a hand across his face. Troubled and sad, he reached for the mug and took a sip of the scalding coffee.

Diane came back into the kitchen. "When you're finished your coffee, I'll drive you home."

Wilfred blew on the coffee to cool it. "How are the kids?"

"Oh, they're fine." She picked up the coffee jar and the sugar from the table and carried them across the room. "Robbie's going into grade twelve this fall, and the girls aren't far behind."

She leaned against the counter, arms crossed, dressed now in jeans and a T-shirt. How young she looked, Wilfred thought, except for her face. Her eyes especially.

She met his glance and held it. Wilfred felt himself blush, and she looked away uneasily.

"I want to talk to you about something." Her voice was quiet, and it seemed to take her some effort to speak. "But not here. Maybe in the truck."

"Sure, we can go now if you want." He gulped more of the coffee, then set it down and got to his feet. "I left the key in the ignition."

She picked up his cup and rinsed it while he waited at the door. When they got in the truck, she made no move to start the motor but sat with her clenched fists resting on her thighs. Her face was turned away from him, and she seemed to be looking at something out the side window.

"I've made up my mind," she said. "I'm leaving him."

Wilfred stared straight ahead at the dark shadow of the house. "Why are you telling me this?"

She turned toward him. "Because you're Jack's oldest friend. Because I thought you would care."

"I do." His voice trembled. "But why now? You're leaving him now, when everything else is changing? He needs you now."

"I've taken care of his needs long enough." She stopped, then spoke more sharply. "Don't lay that on me, Wilfred. If we're talking about who owes who, I think I come out ahead on that one."

She let out her breath in a sigh.

"The kids are old enough — I think we'll be okay. Robbie's almost on his own, and the girls and me will manage."

"Will you move into town?"

"I guess we'll have to — I'll need a job. Jack will probably stay out here as long as he can, maybe Robbie too. So you can still drive him home at night. Some things never change."

There was a long silence.

"Are you sure this is right?" he asked her finally.

She shrugged abruptly, shook her head. "No, of course not. When was I ever sure about anything? Wasn't sure I should marry him in the first place. Wasn't sure we should have kids. Last time I was sure about anything, it was you — and look how that turned out."

Wilfred pressed himself against the seat back, rigid and unmoving. His palms were stretched out on his legs, fingers curled over his knees. "That was a long time ago, Diane."

"Not so long," she said. "Twenty-one years. Sometimes it seems like yesterday."

Wilfred breathed deeply, slowly. He felt the smallness of the cab, how close she was on his left.

"Everything changes," he said. He struggled to control the quaver at the edges of his words. "You have to move on."

"Move on." Her voice turned hard. "You're good at that. Your brother drowns, you move on. You lose me, you move on. Your parents die, you move on. Always moving on."

He lifted his hands from his knees, placed them together and locked his fingers tightly. "What else was there to do? What choice did I have, about any of it? I didn't choose to end it with you."

"You didn't choose to be with me, either."

Wilfred's lips moved, but he was silent. Twenty-one years, he thought, and the old defences and arguments still came to his mind like a long-used tool came to hand.

"Let's not talk about this, Diane," he said finally. "You know what happened, you know what happened to me after Adam drowned. I just couldn't deal with it. I needed more help than anyone here could give me, so they sent me away. I learned to manage. There's nothing else to say."

He heard her draw a long breath, then let it out slowly.

"There's one thing left to say, Wilfred. We could start over now." She made a small, impatient movement with her hand. "I know — neither one of us is what we were. But it could hardly be worse than the past twenty years."

"No," Wilfred said. "It's too late for that."

She hit the steering wheel suddenly with the palm of her hand. "It's not too late — don't tell me it's too late. Damn it, Wilfred, take a chance for once. You're barely alive the way you are."

He turned away from her quickly, felt for the door handle. Her fingers grazed his elbow, then the door was open and he was outside.

"Wilfred, get in."

He didn't look back. "I'll walk," he said, and stepped away from her into the darkness, leaving the pickup door open behind him.

AFTER HE CROSSED the railway tracks, he slowed down and glanced back. She wasn't following him — he had no reason to think that she would.

He forced himself into a steady pace. *One, two*, he counted steps as he inhaled, then exhaled through *three, four, five*. He could pick out the amber of his yard light in the distance. The diagonal route he would follow across the fields was less than three miles. Even in the dark, he'd be home in an hour.

He drew the cool air deeply into his lungs. Out here, it was easier to dismiss what she'd said, even to pretend that her words had not been spoken. The sky glowed above him, wide and close. The earth beneath him seemed less real, veiled in a layer of darkness at his feet.

He thought of the fields he would cross on the way home — the rocky, uneven grassland he was on now, the summerfallow field that belonged to Johnsons, the quarter of pasture he'd sold soon after his father died, his own eighty acres of alfalfa he'd started baling yesterday. Then a short walk through the barley close to the yard.

A badger mound caught his foot, and he stumbled, then stopped to catch his breath. The dull yellow rectangle of an upstairs window was all he could see now of Jack's and Diane's house. A truck geared down on the main highway, the sound coming to him faintly but distinctly over the miles. He had a sudden sense of how few people there were, and of how great the distances were between them.

He turned abruptly and continued walking, counting his steps, breathing in rhythm with his long strides. He kept his eye on the distant light in his yard. He was in the summerfallow now, and his feet sank deeply into the sandy surface. The dry, sharp taste of the soil caught on his tongue and in his nose. Grey vertical lines of cedar posts emerged from the darkness on his left, and he followed the fenceline until it intersected at right angles with a second fence. He pushed down the middle strand of barbed wire and ducked through.

The sky was brightening to the northeast, the deep blue turning paler toward the horizon and streaked lightly with pink. He could see the ground more clearly now. The land he was on, the pasture that had once been his, had never been broken. The dense prairie grasses crunched under his boots, broken by patches of short brush.

He hadn't set foot on this land since he'd sold it, though it was little more than a mile from home. The neighbour he'd offered it to shortly after Wilfred's father died was surprised that he was selling such good pastureland with an unfailing water supply. But he was glad for the opportunity, and didn't press Wilfred for a reason. A creek ran diagonally across the quarter, and where the banks were highest and steepest, an earthen dam had been built. The pond that formed behind the dam was deep and stretched for more than a quarter-mile across the centre of the pasture.

Wilfred could see the water, a shining ribbon of light across his pathway, now just a few hundred yards distant. As he drew nearer, his breath quickened and he felt his chest tighten. His shoulders and upper arms trembled.

He was following a track worn down by cattle hooves that would lead him across the earthen dam. He felt an urge to turn away, to go back, but the only route home that made sense was straight ahead.

"I'll be okay," he said aloud. "I'll be okay. It's all in the past. A long time ago. Nothing to be afraid of." He kept his eyes on the pathway in front of his feet. The water was just ahead on his right, the deep creek bed to his left. He started across the wide top of the dam. He felt lightheaded, and he tried to force more air into his lungs. It seemed to him that the way ahead was narrowing, that the water was inexplicably closer on his right. The hard clay beneath his feet no longer seemed solid, and he was overtaken by the sensation that the pathway was floating on the surface of the water. Desperate to reach the other side, he began to run, and his breath came in gasps. His boots were heavy on his feet, his legs sluggish. He stumbled against a stone and fell, his hands tearing through the tangled low growth beside the path.

He lay still, face down, unable to draw his breath, and gave in to the force of the memory.

It had been early spring. The water behind the dam was open and high. Banks of dirty water-logged snow lined the shore. The overflow rushed through the shallow, rock-lined channel of the spillway at one end of the dam, and down to the creek bed below.

Wilfred was eighteen that spring, Adam was twelve. Through the winter, they'd passed long evenings in the hayloft. By the light of a lantern, they assembled plywood and scraps of hardwood into a snub-nosed eight-foot dinghy. When the ice broke in the spring, they hauled the boat to the dam in the pickup, and pushed it gingerly out from the shore, watching for leaks. When none appeared, they climbed in and used the oars to propel themselves out onto the frigid water.

"Our maiden voyage," Adam laughed. "Without any maidens."

They were cautious at first, but the little boat seemed strong and stable. They circuited the pond a few times, taking turns at the oars. Wilfred felt a deep, quiet pride in their success. The boat rode high and light on the water, and the fresh marine paint shone white on the inside and a deep blue on the outside.

"Let's run the spillway, Wilf," Adam urged after half an hour.

Wilfred resisted at first, but his caution was swept away by Adam's exuberance. They rowed toward the faster moving water, then let the current catch the boat and carry them over the lip of the spillway. There was a short plunge down the narrow channel to a small tailpond that formed in the creek bed just below the dam.

"Wow — that was great!" Adam's cheeks were rosy, and his eyes were wide with excitement. "Let's do it again!"

They dragged the boat over the drifts back up to the pond. Whooping with exhilaration, they rode down the rapids of the spillway again and again, trading a few seconds of heady excitement for the long haul up to the pond. Soon their pantlegs were soaked, and their lungs ached with the exertion.

On their final descent through the spillway, Wilfred heard a dull scrape of wood against stone, and felt the boat lurch sharply to the side. But they were soon through the rapids, and began to drag the dinghy up along what was now a well-worn path.

"Just one more," Wilfred panted. "Then we better get home before our feet start to freeze."

They pushed the bow of the boat out onto the water. They were both tired now. While Wilfred held the stern from the shore, Adam climbed in and took the oars. With one foot in the boat, Wilfred kicked off from shore with the other, and then took a seat in the back. Adam began to row.

Suddenly, behind Adam, Wilfred saw yellow-black water gushing through a break in the bow.

"Get back!" he yelled.

The crack gave way, and the bow dropped below the surface. Adam fell back into the water with a cry of shock. Wilfred saw him lose hold of the oars, saw his arms thrash as he went under — then the stern went down and he was in the water himself. He felt the weight of the water dragging at his clothes, and he clung to the wooden gunwale. He came up with the boat, and kicked desperately to shore, tearing his hands on the rocks as he dragged himself to safety.

There was nothing to be seen of Adam. Wilfred screamed his name, and scanned the dark surface of the water desperately. A paddle floated toward shore and Wilfred grabbed for it. He called out again, then stood helpless and silent, watching for some sign of life that never came.

IN THE HALF LIGHT of early morning, Wilfred crossed his yard and entered the house. He ran water in the tub and undressed. Mud had dried where his face had been wet with tears, and his hands stung with tiny thorns.

He bathed carefully. He took tweezers from a drawer and pulled each thorn, holding his hands close to the light. He dressed in clean clothes, then sat at the kitchen table. Sunlight moved across the drawn blinds, its light direct and white at midday, then turning amber toward the evening. He ate nothing. At times during the day, he thought of the baler than needed to be repaired, and the eggs waiting to be gathered. But he couldn't find the will to move.

His hands lay on the table in front of him. He began to move them in small symmetrical figures, one hand's pattern a mirror image of the other's. His hands started, changed directions, stopped, and moved again, tracing square upon square as the light faded from the room.

Correction Line

THE WEATHERED PLYWOOD SIGN THAT I REMEMBER FROM CHILDhood still marks the turnoff to Kildeer Lake Bible Camp. A few hundred yards off Highway 9, the access road degenerates to a narrow track across semi-arid ranchland. Maintained with a pass or two of a grader each year, the road is little more than a strip of sandy soil scraped bare, with sod piled at the sides and the occasional diagonal ridge where the blade of the grader bumped over a rock.

Each year when my parents drove me to camp, a growing sense of what I would now call desolation came over me as soon as we started down that dusty road, a feeling that matched what I observed beyond the windows of the car. Ten minutes off the highway, a Texas gate rattled under the wheels, and then there was nothing to be seen to the south but a long, indistinct horizon, with a deserted farm site to the southeast, and to the southwest the cluster of buildings that marked the camp.

At the campground, two short rows of what looked like castoff wooden granaries were designated as boys' and girls' cabins. A larger building, covered with painted green plywood, housed a chapel, a dining hall, and a kitchen. The most prominent feature was the ball diamond, with its tall chicken wire backstop. The campground was surrounded by a barbed wire fence to keep out the curious cattle that at times wandered close by. Kildeer Lake itself hadn't held any water past June for as long as anyone could remember. But the foxtail always grew abundantly, and not far outside the camp fence was an alkali-laced stretch of sand we called the beach.

When I was ten, after I'd been going to camp for three or four years, Lyle McDonald came to Kildeer Lake for the first time, and we were assigned to the same cabin with six other boys. Lyle lived in Sheerness then, before his father was injured at the mine and the family moved into town. Sheerness was a tiny coal-mining village, and the Sheerness boys had a reputation for trouble.

From the time the wake-up bell rang at six-thirty until lights out at ten-thirty, the camp ran by a schedule designed to allow little room for devilry and disorder. But there was about half an hour free time between supper dishes and the evening campfire. Robbie Harmon, a kid from a ranch close to the Red Deer River, snared a gopher with his shoelace and brought it into our cabin. The gopher was tugging frantically on the end of the string and squealing.

"You can get bubonic plague from them things," Eldon Siemens said, eyeing the gopher from a distance. Eldon went to my church, and like his father, he thought he'd been put on earth to share his superior knowledge about any subject that you could raise. "You see them spots on it, them black marks? It's got the black death."

"The hell it does." Lyle looked down from the top bunk where he was carving something into the two-by-four side rail. He snapped the knife closed and jumped down. "Give me that thing," he said. "I'll show you black death."

Even at ten years of age, Lyle's mouth was set in a permanent sneer. He was lean and tanned, and he never seemed to move any faster than he needed to. He was small like me, but next to him I felt insignificant, short and pudgy and clumsy, with a complexion that was always too pink.

Lyle took the end of the shoelace from Robbie and looped it a couple of times around the leg of a chair, pulling it tighter until the gopher was snugged up close to the leg so it couldn't move. He got up and reached under his mattress, and his hand came out with a pack of cigarettes and some matches. Right away, I could feel my chest getting tight, and it seemed hard to keep breathing.

"If any you Jesus boys rats on me," he said, looking around at us, "you'll be crucified for sure."

As sure of himself as if he'd been born smoking, Lyle stuck a cigarette in the corner of his mouth and lit it, then exhaled long and slow. He put the cigarettes and the matches back under his mattress, then knelt down on the plywood floor. He moved the lit end of the cigarette toward the gopher, and when it felt the heat it jerked away hard, pulling the chair about half an inch along the floor.

"Shit," Robbie said, sounding scared.

I opened my mouth and heard myself saying, "Let him go or I'll tell."

Lyle looked at me, and took a long drag on the cigarette. "You'll be next, Wiens." he said, and his lip curled with disgust. "*Wiener* Wiens." The rest of the guys laughed at that, and Lyle started poking the cigarette toward the gopher again.

The door opened and in walked Mr. Blair, our cabin counselor. He stopped, and all of us froze while he took in the scene. His expression changed from surprise to anger. He grabbed Lyle by the back of his collar, snatched the cigarette out of his hand and ground it out against the floor.

"Just what do you think you're doing?" he said, his voice tight. He pulled harder on Lyle's collar, and Lyle's heels lifted off the floor. Lyle's arms started to come up toward his head, as if he thought he was about to be hit. Then Mr. Blair let go of him and looked around at all of us. He took a deep breath and let it out with a tired-sounding sigh.

"Somebody get the gopher out of here," he said, and Robbie

started to drag the chair toward the door. "And kill the poor bugger. He's half-choked and scared to death anyway."

That night, coming back to our cabin after the campfire, Lyle came up behind me in the dark. "You better say your prayers, Wiener," he whispered. "I'm going to string you up like that gopher and slit your throat."

I believed him. For the rest of camp, I stayed as far away from Lyle McDonald as I could. I did my best to avoid him for years afterward too. But the nickname he gave me that summer wasn't as easy to shake. By the time Lyle and I became friends, about eight years later, only the adults in my life called me Gerald. To everyone else I was Wiener, and that was the name I preferred.

IT'S TAKEN ME SOME TIME to recognize that what happened in the last few months of high school had an enduring influence on who I've become, how I think and feel. That's especially true of my short-lived friendship with Lyle, which was rooted in the choice of one impulsive moment.

One day in the early spring of that year, I was at my locker trying to find my books before math class. Close to me I heard someone swear, and a grunt. I turned to see Ray Beck, one of the biggest guys from my class, slam Lyle up against the lockers on the other side of the hall. Everybody jumped back to clear a space for them. Their faces were close, and their eyes bright with rage. Ray went for Lyle's crotch with his knee, and Lyle twisted to protect himself, trying to get a thumb in Ray's eye. Ray pulled back for a second, but then he butted Lyle hard with his head, and Lyle's nose spurted blood.

Maybe it was the blood that made Lyle seem helpless and made me lose my head. Whatever it was, I found myself in the middle of it, pushing Ray back. Lucky for me, the principal arrived suddenly, sweating in his tight blue suit, his face red. He ordered everybody to get to class. Somebody brought Lyle a wet paper towel for his nose, and I went off with my pulse racing, wondering what Lyle

McDonald had ever done to deserve my help.

A few days later, I was waiting for the bus out in front of the school when Lyle came by. He was wearing sunglasses, but I could see the bruises around his eyes, and his nose was swollen and shiny.

He looked at me and nodded. "Ray says to thank you for saving his life."

"Saving the life of your children, more like it," I said, and laughed. "Of course, with a face like that, it might be a long time before you're getting any." I still had the same stupid mouth I had when I was ten.

Lyle eyed me for a minute from behind his shades, and then he grinned. "Could be right about that."

I grinned back, relieved.

LYLE BOUGHT A MOTORCYCLE that spring, a Yamaha 750. The first day he brought it to school, we all circled around it at noon hour in the parking lot. We didn't say much, but it made us crazy being that close to it and not being able to take it for a ride. Lyle came out of the school carrying his helmet, and he looked around at us.

"Eat your fuckin' hearts," he said, quiet and kind of satisfied. He swung his leg over the bike and buckled on his helmet. Then he looked at me. "Hey, Wiener. For once you want to have something big and fast between your legs?"

The guys started laughing, but they stopped when they saw Lyle was handing the spare helmet to me. I took it, buckled it on, and climbed onto the bike behind Lyle. By the time we were out of town and on Highway 9, I was through being nervous. I felt I was right at the centre of something, right where I wanted to be, with the black road rushing by so close I could have touched it with my feet. The prairie spread out around us somehow bigger and greener than it had ever been any spring before. My head was full of the sound of the wind and the motor, and I felt the life of the bike coming through my thighs. And in front of me was Lyle, hunched over in his leather jacket, and I imagined him grinning so big I could almost see it through the back of his helmet.

After that, we started playing pool together. I'd grab my lunch from the locker after the last class in the morning, and we'd ride Lyle's bike down to the pool hall. I'd never played pool much before that, but Lyle seemed to like to show me what he knew. I liked the pool hall too — dark and quiet in the middle of the day, with the wood floor creaking and the only light coming from the fluorescents above the tables and the windows way down at the far end.

It wasn't long until my parents heard what I was doing with my noon hours, and who I was doing it with. "What's this about you hanging around the pool hall at lunch time?" my mother said, making sure my dad was around to back her up.

"I'm not hanging around," I said. "We're playing pool — there's nothing wrong with that."

"It's not the playing pool we're concerned about, Gerald," my father said. His head was tipped back a bit so he could watch me through the strong part of his bifocals, as if I were a book he was trying to read. "It's the atmosphere of the place, and who you're with."

"What's wrong with Lyle?" I asked. As soon as the question was out, I knew I'd given him too much of an opening.

"Well," my father said, and both of his eyebrows went way up. "You'll remember he got sent to Bowden for stealing the principal's car. He comes from a broken home. His father's a drinker. From what I hear, he's been charged with possession of alcohol himself once or twice. And there's that motorcycle."

"So which one of the commandments covers motorcycles?" I could hear the belligerence in my voice, and I wished I could take it back.

My dad didn't say anything for a while, just peered at me with an expression that was on the edge of amusement. Then he turned away, and glanced at my mom. "He's probably not a good influence," he said. "But that's a choice you're going to have to make for yourself, I suppose."

Mom grimaced a bit in Dad's direction, but seemed to be ready to let it go. I'd been braced for an argument, and I felt relieved and let down all at the same time.

I WAS OUT ON FOOT the next Saturday, fixing the fence around the big pasture, when I heard Lyle's Yamaha a long way off. He was gunning it through the hollows in first gear, coming toward me across the field. I was surprised to see him, and curious. He hadn't been out to our place before, and whenever I'd talked about my family, I had the impression he wasn't that eager to meet them. I watched him as he came closer, his legs spread out wide to keep his balance.

"How'd you find me?" I asked when he pulled up and shut off the motor. The bike was coated with a fine grey dust, so heavy it ran off the gas tank in tiny streams.

"Your old man drew me a map," he said. "Nothing to it."

He heaved the bike back on the stand, got off, and hung his helmet on the handlebars. "So what are you doing — building a fence?"

"Just checking to make sure the wires are on tight," I told him, "and fixing it where it needs fixing."

He picked up the fencing pliers from the toolbox. "Look at the snout on these things," he said. "I'd like to have old Ray's balls in there."

He looked around, like there should be something more to see. "What can I do?"

I showed him how to check where the barbed wire was fastened to the posts, and how to refasten it where it had come loose. He took a hammer and half the staples, rode down to the southeast corner of the pasture, and started working back toward me. Once he got started, he seemed to think about nothing but the work ahead of him. Whenever I looked, he was bent over at a post, and

I could hear the impact of his hammer, a bit out of time with his swing because of the distance across the field. We finished the three miles of fence before suppertime, and headed home on the bike, me balancing the greasy wooden toolbox across my knees.

Dad was in the quonset when I put the tools away.

"So how'd you do?" he asked. He looked skeptical, probably thinking Lyle had been more of a distraction than anything.

I told him we were finished, and his expression changed. "Lyle was a big help," I said. "He worked hard."

By the way he moved his mouth, I could see my dad was working hard himself, trying to make some adjustments in his view of Lyle. "Is he staying for supper?" he said finally.

"I'll ask him."

We all went into the house, and while Lyle was in the bathroom washing up I heard my mother say in a quiet voice to my dad, "So he's eating with us, is he?"

"Can't very well have him working all afternoon and not feed him," my father replied.

Mom set another place. I could tell she wasn't very happy about it — her mouth was tight and pulled down in one corner. But when Lyle came into the kitchen, she said, "They've been putting you to work, have they?" in a cheerful voice.

"Wasn't doing much, Mrs. Wiens," Lyle said. "Just walking around."

"Well, I'm sure you're hungry anyway."

He didn't answer, but he kept watching the food as if he was afraid that it might disappear.

We sat down, Lyle and me on one side, my little brother Aaron and little sister Anola on the other, and my parents at the ends. There was a home-grown rib roast and gravy, with mashed potatoes and peas and a carrot salad with raisins in it. There were beet pickles and bread too, that my mother cut in crooked thick slices. Not all the dishes matched, and the yellow oilcloth on the table was getting old, worn almost white where it hung over the edge of the table.

Lyle knew enough not to dive in, maybe the one thing he learned at Bible camp.

"Heavenly father," my father prayed, sounding slow and thoughtful, "we thank thee for thy goodness to us and the blessings of your hand. Bless this food to the strengthening of our bodies, and us in thy service. For Jesus' sake. Amen."

Then we ate. Lyle seemed careful at first, waiting for the serving dishes to come by and watching to see how much I took. I put a big spoonful of horseradish on my meat and spread it around, and Lyle did the same.

"You like that stuff?" I asked, when he was taking his first mouthful.

He chewed for a while, and his face reddened. "Not much," he said, and started scraping it to the side of his plate. Anola watched him and giggled. "You want my horseradish, Anola?" he said, and she giggled more.

Aaron started talking to Lyle about his bike. "Must be pretty good on gas," Aaron said. He told Lyle about the Indian motorcycle that Uncle Albert had, and how it had pedals to get you to the next station if you ever ran out of gas.

I started to tune out, while the voices and the sounds of eating went on around me. The food came by, and I filled my plate again. Right then, everything about life seemed good. Even the colours on my plate, dark reds, greens, and deep browns, seemed to fit together just right. The light through the window was getting low and yellow as the shadows of the poplars fell across the house, and the old tablecloth glowed.

Dessert got my attention. Mom cut pieces of saskatoon pie, thick and warm, and set the plates in front of my dad. Dad scooped ice cream onto the pie, taking his time like it was his only job and he was going to make sure he got it right. When he was finished, he gave one to me.

"Here, Gerald, hand that down to your friend."

"It's the biggest piece," I said. "Lyle, you got the biggest piece."

"What's wrong, Dad?" Aaron said. "You usually take the biggest piece yourself."

"I don't know about that," Dad said, and Mom jumped in with, "Oh, yes, you do!"

Lyle had already taken a few mouthfuls, probably to make sure we weren't going to take it back.

LATE IN MAY, Lyle's mother moved back to town. He hadn't heard a word from her in two years, and one day she came around to the school to see him and the next day moved back in with his father. From a distance she looked slim and young in her tight jeans. Up close, her face looked worn and careful.

We started riding out to the town dam at lunch time. The trees were turning nice and green, and it felt good to be outside. Some days Lyle brought along a mickey of rye in his saddlebag. I didn't like it much, but I would put some in my coke just to be sociable. Lyle drank straight from the bottle, and after a while he would give up trying to get me to drink. The thing with Lyle was that he didn't talk a lot when he drank, he usually got even more into himself. He'd stop laughing at my stories, and he would just sit there looking at the water. Sometimes I thought he'd forgotten I was there at all.

"I gotta get out of this town," he said one day after about half an hour of doing nothing but drinking and throwing stones at a bottle that was floating in the dam.

"So who doesn't?" I said.

"Yeah, but I got reasons."

I let that be for a minute, but he didn't seem to be taking it anywhere, so I prompted him a little. "Which are?"

"Jesus, Wiener!" he said. "I'm flunking out of high school. I've done time. I've got a fucked-up excuse for an old man and old lady who don't have the sense to quit beating on each other or to stay apart. This town's got me pegged for a loser."

"You're not a loser in my books," I managed.

"Not in mine either," he said, quiet. He took a long drink. "Besides, I'm eighteen, and it's time to be on my own. What reason have I got to stay?"

I'd had enough rye to think, *You've got your buddy Wiener,* but not enough to come right out and say it.

ON THE FACE OF IT, life doesn't seem that hard to understand. But then something happens that peels back the surface, and you never again see the world the way it used to be.

Lyle pulled into the yard one night when it was almost dark. He stopped his bike over by the fuel tanks, and I went out.

"I'm low on gas," he said, "and this thing doesn't have any pedals."

"All we got is purple," I told him.

Lyle shrugged. "Runs fine on grape anyway."

I unlocked the hose and handed it to him, then I twisted open the valve on the end of the tank. He straddled the bike while he filled up, peering in to make sure the tank didn't overflow. When it was full he handed the hose back to me.

"What you been up to?" I asked him.

"Just riding," he said. "Better than being at home."

He pulled a rag out of his pocket and tried to clean the bugs off his visor. "Want to come riding?"

"Naw — I've got some homework to finish up. I'll see you tomorrow."

He started up and circled out of the yard, the light from his headlight sweeping across the side of the quonset and then the house. Then there was nothing but his tail light disappearing down the driveway.

EARLY THE NEXT MORNING I was in the pasture. I'd rounded up the cows, and had started chasing them toward home to be milked, swinging an old willow fencepost in my hand. Our old International pickup came over the hill, and I could see that it was my brother Aaron. He circled wide to avoid spooking the cows and came toward me. The truck's suspension made a hollow sound as the wheels thumped through the rough spots, and the chains on the tailgate rattled. When he pulled up alongside, I noticed the look on his face. It was almost like a smile, but hesitant, and his eyes had a strange brightness to them. He didn't seem to know what he wanted to say at first.

"Lyle McDonald had an accident last night," he said after a few seconds. "Missed the corner at the correction line north of Andersons and ended up in a rock pile."

"He's dead," I said.

"Yeah." Aaron looked away. "Want to get in?" he asked after some silence. "We can chase the cows home with the truck."

"No, you go," I said. "I'll bring them home on foot."

I started off toward the back of the herd, now a hundred yards distant. Every step I took seemed separate and planned, as if I had suddenly forgotten how to walk.

PEOPLE LIKE TO SAY the prairies are like fabric stretched out on a quilting frame, with all the square fields stitched together and laid flat from horizon to horizon. The squares are a mile each way, and thirty-six of these squares make a bigger square, measuring six miles east to west and north to south. Each bigger square has a township number and a range number, and by the time they were seven or eight farm kids used to know their land description as well as they knew their phone number. For me it was the southwest quarter of section six, township thirty-three, range thirteen, west of the fourth meridian.

Maybe that's why I thought I knew my exact place in the universe, in a way that a street name and number could never account for. A surveyor's map is as clear and logical as the graph paper in math class, with X and Y co-ordinates to match any place you happen to put your pencil down.

But of course it's not that simple — because the world isn't flat or square-cornered at all. When the survey crews marked it out, as my father would tell me, they had to find a way to compensate for the curvature of the earth. It's as if you were stacking square bales inside a huge quonset with sides that gradually curve in tighter and tighter. The farther up you go, the less room there is from side to side. The farther north, the less distance there is east to west. So every twenty-four miles, the surveyors had to jog a bit to the side — a correction line, they called it.

Late one night in June you're driving on some back road, and you think it could go on forever, roads and road allowances like a long seam running straight on up through the province. Even when the open spaces and the farms run out, somewhere past Edmonton, you think maybe the line keeps on going, like an invisible mark scored in the air, just above the treetops and the tundra and the pack ice. All the way to the North Pole.

Then you hit the hollow a half-mile past the Anderson place, doing eighty-five miles an hour and you don't slow down because the road is smooth, not much gravel, and the rise on the other side is gradual. You come up the slope and there not fifty yards in front of you is a faded-out checkerboard sign and the road disappearing at right angles to the east and west. Maybe it's the rye, or maybe it's just a quick thought as clear and dark as the night sky — that it's too late for the brakes, that your chances are better straight ahead in the field. A half-second later your headlight catches the grey posts and the black wire of the fence, and just beyond that, obscured by wild roses and buckbrush, a low pile of rocks.

Correction line.

THE FIRST SUNDAY after I'd finished writing exams, I told my parents that I didn't feel well and stayed home while everyone else went to church. When they were gone, I took the truck and drove the few miles to the place where Lyle had died.

I parked the half-ton on the road, and left the door open. The tracks in the ditch were still visible, marking where the RCMP and the ambulance pulled in, too late. The fence had been fixed. The new green pressure-treated posts looked out of place. I squeezed through the tight wires of the fence, and stepped up onto the rock pile. There could still be blood somewhere, I thought, but under my feet were only the pink mottled shapes of smooth granite and rough, irregular grey boulders, streaked white with bird droppings.

I lowered myself onto my knees, and then lay prone on the rocks. I smelled cow manure and grass, and I heard the sound of a meadowlark and the thin, never-ending breath of the wind. A sharp edge of rock pressed against my hipbone, and another into my ribs. I felt the heaviness of my body, pushing against an unyielding planet. Helpless and ashamed, I hid my face in the space between two rocks and cried.

TEN YEARS AFTER I graduated from high school, my parents sold the farm and bought a house in town. They were young to retire, but by then my siblings and I had made it clear that none of us was interested in taking over the farm, and they got a good price for the land.

I went home the first Thanksgiving weekend after my parents moved. The house in town seemed too bright and orderly, and I felt restless and out of place. After dinner on Sunday, my father suggested that the two of us take a walk, and we headed north out of town. As we followed the gravel road we talked lightly about the year's harvest and of the families who lived in the few houses that we passed along the way. The sky was an intense cold blue, darker than the skies of summer, with high, compact clouds.

A half-mile out of town, a white wrought-iron arch marked the entrance to the cemetery. I was about to keep walking, but my father turned in.

"We just bought our plots," he said. "Come and have a look."

"Aren't you a little young for that?" I felt resentful at another reminder of change. I followed him reluctantly to a new section of the cemetery where there were few headstones. At the top of a small hill, he pointed out their gravesites. He seemed pleased.

"It's a good view," I said, a bit sarcastically. The houses and elevators of town were spread out to the south. To the southwest, perhaps twenty miles distant, the line of the Hand Hills was sharply drawn against the fall sky. I watched for a moment, then turned around to look back across the older part of the cemetery.

"Lyle MacDonald is buried here," I said.

We were both silent.

It's the land that holds our memories, I thought, the land that keeps the fragments of our past within reach, even when we'd rather forget. And it's the land that brings our stories to life again when we need to recover what we once left behind.

"Let's go," my father said. "We don't want to be late for supper."

He began to walk briskly toward the road. I hesitated, unsure if I should visit Lyle's grave. In that moment, I didn't know what to say to my father, or if I stayed, how to tell him that I needed to be alone. I took a last quick look at the place where my father and mother would one day be buried, then turned to follow him home.

The Bottom Half of Empty

EVERETT STRUGGLED TO FOCUS ON THE RED NUMERALS OF THE clock radio. Three-thirty. He was just awake, but he'd been uncomfortable and restless for some time. The mattress was hard, and the pillow thin and flat. He swung his feet to the floor and switched on the bedside lamp. He retrieved his dress pants from the chair and pulled them on, then took a golf shirt from his overnight bag.

The few hours he'd spent inside these four cinder-block walls at the Hitching Post Motel in Mankota were enough, more than enough. He took a business card from the pocket of his leather jacket, printed "checked out early — please fax receipt" on the blank side, and left it with the key on top of the television.

He started the Cherokee, and saw that the gas gauge showed less than a quarter tank. The Petro-Can sign down the street was lit up, but at this time of night, in a town of a couple hundred, he knew it would be closed. He hesitated only a moment before turning onto the roadway and accelerating hard toward the outskirts of town. He probably didn't have enough fuel to get to Assiniboia, certainly not all the way home to Regina. But there was no sense in turning back now. The key was locked inside the motel room, and he wouldn't have returned even if he could.

"What's this one about, Everett?" he asked out loud.

He recognized the pattern. His life had been punctuated at long intervals by solitary drives and walks; there were questions he seemed unable to work out if he stayed in one place. It was mostly about Aimee, he knew that at least. He'd left her high school grad just a few hours earlier, and now he felt unsettled, almost agitated. He'd expected something different from the occasion, a sense that this part of life had been neatly wrapped up. Instead, he found himself feeling that nothing had been resolved, that he had slipped back to a time when his emotions were raw and his wounds fresh.

WHEN SHE WAS THIRTEEN, Aimee asked to move into the basement bedroom.

"It's dark down there," he'd objected. "And cold."

"That's okay. I'm tired of the whole sunshiny, frilly curtains thing anyway."

So they helped her redecorate and move. Instead of the carpet that he and Susan suggested, Aimee wanted to paint the concrete floor a deep cobalt blue. They panelled the walls with unfinished plywood edged with metal drywall bead, and installed industrial-type light fixtures, bare incandescent bulbs in wire cages.

"Admit it, Dad," she said when they'd finished. "You'd never let me do this to my old room upstairs."

"You're right," he told her. "It looks like somebody's workshop." But he secretly liked the effect, and saw how pleased she was.

He wasn't as happy with the changes she made to her own look that year. As if to suit the décor of her room, she began wearing studded bracelets and metal chains, and what looked to Everett like work boots. He found the contents of one of his small toolboxes on his workbench one day, and discovered that Aimee was using it as a purse. After a couple of months of arguments and objections, mostly on his part rather than Susan's, she had her eyebrow pierced.

"You're starting to rattle when you walk, like Morley's ghost," he said, trying to be good humoured.

But there was something about Aimee's transformation that made Everett uneasy and afraid — the way she seemed to have stopped looking at him, the way her eyes shifted to the side or focused in the distance. Her gaze had always been alive, direct. She was still that way with her friends, but not with her parents.

After she moved out, they left her room as it was. Months later, Everett found himself standing at her dresser, opening and closing the empty drawers. He spotted a folded paper in a back corner of one of them, opened it, and was startled when he recognized his own handwriting.

My dear Aimee, the note began. *Perhaps some day you will have a daughter of your own, and then you will understand how much I love you, and how hard it is to see you go.*

He pushed the drawer closed and sat on the edge of her bed, the paper in his hand. His note was one of the few things she'd left behind, he realized suddenly. The anger and fear he'd tried to ignore for months returned to him like a tightening band around his chest, and along with it a hunger for her presence that was stronger than he'd ever felt before. He ripped the paper in half, then tore it again and again until the fragments lay around his feet, like white leaves against the cold, dark surface of the concrete floor.

SHE WAS THEIR ONLY CHILD. They had planned and waited for her eagerly, impatiently, and when Susan had discovered she was pregnant, she decided to quit the bank job she had then and stay home. He'd questioned her decision, reminding her of what the loss of income would mean.

"This matters more," she said. "At least to me it does." And he'd come to agree with her.

Through Aimee's early years, he and Susan had often marvelled to each other that she surpassed the sum of her parents' best attributes. She was more confident, more expressive, more open, less anxious. From her first years at school, she attracted a diverse group of friends — "the motley crew" he'd taken to calling them. When he came home from work to find a tangled pile of shoes in the doorway, he'd call out, "Greetings, Motley Crew," proud of the way his daughter accepted everyone, and received the same in return. He felt that he was somehow a part of that circle, and that he always would be.

After supper on her thirteenth birthday, Susan told Aimee to sit beside him on the couch while she took a photograph. As he reached to pull her close, he felt her shoulder, uncomfortably high and hard under his arm.

"We never do this anymore," he joked, and he felt her pull away from him a little as the camera flashed. No goodnight hugs either, he realized. He tried to remember when they'd stopped. He wasn't sure which of them had made the change, or if either of them had made any conscious choice at all. At times now, he wondered if he had been the one who first began to withdraw.

EARLIER THAT EVENING, with the others in her class, she'd come down off the stage in the high school gym with a rose in her hand and found him in the crowd. She slipped into his arms without hesitation, kissed his cheek.

"Thanks, Dad," she said lightly, but without a trace of falseness. "For everything you've put up with."

"Aw, you're worth it all," he replied, trying to be gruff. He watched her as she pushed a wisp of hair back from her face. She seemed suddenly adult, and he wondered how it had happened so quickly.

Later, after the speeches and the diplomas, he filed out through the folding metal chairs into the hallway. Someone whose face was familiar but whose name he'd forgotten nodded to him.

"So, Everett, how's life in the city?" he asked, eyeing him skeptically.

"Not much of a city, as cities go," Everett replied, hearing a drawl insinuate itself into his voice. "Maybe not much of a life, either."

The other man looked away. "It's not for me. Never know when your car's going to get stolen, or when you're going to wake up at night with some young buck standing over your bed with a knife."

Everett was suddenly irritated, wanting the conversation to end. "It's not just the city. What about that couple murdered up in Kyle last month?"

"Sure, Everett," he snorted quietly. "And where were those kids from who did the killing? Besides, if the city's so great, what's your daughter doing here?"

Aimee approached while he was trying to think of a reply. He turned to her, relieved, and the other man walked away. "I guess I'll go now, Dad. Did you talk to Mom tonight?"

"Yes, I did." Her father had suffered a stroke two days earlier, and she had flown home to Winnipeg to be with him and her mother. "She told me to tell you how much she wishes she could be here. She says she'll find a way to make it up to you."

Her face became tense with worry. "How's Grandpa doing?"

"Improving," he said. He wanted to reassure her, dispel the cloud that had descended over the evening. "His speech seems to be coming back today."

"It's hard to think of him as old," she said. "I mean, he's always been old, but this is different."

"He'll be okay," Everett said, without conviction. "Don't worry about him tonight."

She looked at him carefully. It was the look she'd given him as a child when he was explaining something to her — attentive, but skeptical.

A tall, lean boy moved up beside her, and she introduced him. He seemed bored and restless.

"Come on, Aim," he said, and pulled her hand. He started to move away.

She seemed reluctant to leave. "Are you staying over at Grandma and Grandpa's?"

"No," he told her. "I told them I was heading back, but I'll probably hang around here for a while, and then get a room down in Mankota. How about you? Big party tonight after the dance?"

"Yeah," she said, unenthusiastically, he thought. "In a field somewhere. It's what they always do here, but I guess you'd know."

"Some things don't change," he said. He looked past her at the knots of people leaning together to hear each other's words over the noise. "You should get back to your friends." He put his hand on her shoulder, and kissed her cheek.

"Be careful," he said. Then, trying for a lighter note, "Don't get that dress dirty out there tonight."

Her mouth tightened briefly. "I'll change, Dad," she said impatiently, as if to a child, then started moving away.

Of course, he thought. But some kind of warning was in order, or did he have anything to left to offer on a night like this?

He'd hoped to run into old friends, get invited to someone's house, maybe drink a few beer and talk about old times. But when the dance began, the few he knew waved and greeted him from a distance, or sat down in tight clusters around the tables at one end of the gym. By eleven, he was on his way to the motel, exhausted and unsettled. For a moment, he imagined he could see himself as others must see him, as someone who had become a stranger in what was once his home.

OFF THE ROAD to the south, he saw the scattered lights of McCord. The fuel gauge was barely above empty now, and he briefly considered passing the night parked at the pumps at the Co-op, but kept driving instead. A part of him knew it was foolish, but it was a mild June night, and he felt like driving. At worst, he'd spend a few hours in the Cherokee until someone came by.

"It doesn't cost any more to keep the top half full," his father used to say when he had his first car at sixteen and could never afford more than a few dollars' worth of gas. He smiled to himself, remembering the time his father borrowed his car to go to the post office in town, and returned indignant because he'd had to stop for fuel.

"I know," Everett had cut him off, "it doesn't cost any more to keep the top half full."

"Top half nothing!" his father sputtered. "Now you're running on the bottom half of empty!"

Even now, the memory made him laugh aloud, especially since the story still got a rise out of his father.

He had passed half a lifetime trying not to be like his father, who was serious about everything, always right, mostly silent, and unfailingly sensible. But there were moments when he felt possessed by his father's genes, like time-released DNA. He'd hear himself muttering "my shattered nerves" in his father's voice or catch his own feet moving involuntarily the way his father's did when he was engrossed in reading a book.

But despite his fears, he wasn't becoming his father. His daughter and his wife probably deserved the credit for that. They found ways to let him know that his control was an illusion, that his rational way of looking at things was little more than a pretense.

AFTER AIMEE MOVED OUT, Susan changed her name to Susanna. Then Susanna went back to work, not at the bank, but as community relations manager for a string of fast food restaurants in the city. Susanna had a new name and a new life, and she loved both of them. She told him about her work every night, about the events she sponsored, ads she placed, speeches she made at service clubs, news releases she wrote.

"I miss Aimee," she said one night, six months into her new career. "Sometimes. But I'm having a great time. It's so much fun to be more than a mom again."

Somehow, Susan-become-Susanna had surveyed the shaken-up pieces of their lives and saw new possibilities. She'd taken the loss and turned it into raw energy. Watching her, Everett thought he saw someone who knew the pathway of her life as surely as if it had been marked out with lights.

But he feared at times that he had lost his way. At the publicly-owned gas company where he'd worked since university, he'd been offered a position in a new department christened the Solutions Group. But he'd been baffled by the strange mix of marketing and engineering that was the hallmark of the department, and opted to remain a simple engineer. Now he found himself in what felt to be a career backwater, while younger, more ambitious colleagues enthused about adding value, and developing customer-oriented energy solutions. He could use an energy solution himself.

His wheel dropped off a broken edge of pavement, and bits of asphalt clattered off the undercarriage of the Cherokee. He moved to the left, straddling the centre line of the narrow strip of pavement, hoping to miss the worst of the holes. Even in the middle of the road, the asphalt heaved up in places, wrinkled like weathered tarpaper or broken into chunks the size of curling stones.

Was it Aimee who wore him down? he wondered. The pace of life through his thirties? Or was he like this rundown highway, able to withstand only so many years and heavy loads before it all started to give and break apart?

A FEW MONTHS AFTER Aimee had moved in with her grandparents, Everett's mother called on a Sunday afternoon.

"There's something your father and I want to talk to you about," she said. She spoke for both of them. His father didn't like to talk, especially on the phone.

"Trouble already?" he'd asked.

"She wouldn't go to church with us today." His mother's voice sounded petulant, slightly childish.

"We'd prefer you didn't push her," he said. "Give her some time to work out some more basic issues."

"What could be more basic than that?" she replied, sounding hurt. "Maybe if you'd pushed a little more yourself she'd be home with you now."

"That could be true." Her words stung, but he could almost believe that she was right. "I'm saying that if you get her back up now, nobody's going to win. Give her some time to get settled in. Time to think about changing some of her ways."

His mother paused. He sensed some acquiescence in her silence. "We always made you kids go every Sunday," she said. "Never did you any harm."

"I know, Mom. But times have changed." It didn't do us as much good as you imagine, he wanted to add.

He'd been compliant as a child, eager to avoid confrontation. So he'd gone to church with his family, believed the right things, just as he had gone to school and studied hard. After he left home he kept up the pattern, surprised to discover how much his desire for his parents' approval drove him as an adult. He'd met Susan at church and they attended services together, before they were married and after. But the sense persisted that this didn't quite fit him, that he was being dishonest, that his religious habits were fraudulent.

It was suffering that made his faith real. Until the trouble with Aimee began, his life was relatively easy and tranquil. The nights she didn't come home, he paced the house, breathless with anxiety and anger. The first time she showed up at the door drunk, she refused Susan's help with a vicious rage in her voice that made her seem a different person. He experienced the awful sense of having lost someone irretrievably, something he'd never felt before. It was a deep, helpless terror. If your child could become a stranger, even while living at home, was there anything that you couldn't lose?

He felt a pain so immediate and raw that it took him apart, reduced him to living on the torn edge of his emotion. It was a kind of death. No longer could he map out his life, and then count on his ability to follow the way he'd planned for himself and his family. All he could do was take what the day brought. It was frightening to relinquish control, but it was exhilarating too, like driving too fast at night for the reach of your headlights. Trusting the darkness.

In the midst of his pain, he began to become alive to pleasure in a new way. Even on the worst days, he was surprised by an insistent sense of how good life was. As if he could only now perceive them for what they were, ordinary things became remarkable — the taste of beer, the russet-coloured fescue in the ditches beside the highway, the halo of spring light around the yellow-green of emerging leaves. At times while at work, many hours after sex and despite a long shower in the morning, he'd suddenly catch a trace of Susan's scent, and be overcome with both contentment and desire.

Familiar expressions of faith began to take on a weight of meaning beyond their words. The first lines of the creed, "I believe in God the Father Almighty, maker of heaven and earth, and in Jesus Christ his only Son," seemed perfect, indisputable in their beauty. He found himself silently repeating the Lord's Prayer, finding comfort and mystery in the time-worn rhythm of the words.

GRAD SUPPER had been served in the curling rink. He sat with his parents on one side, and a neighbour of theirs on the other. The head table for the grads and their escorts was decorated with balloons and streamers.

"Just the same menu as at your graduation," his mother observed. "Except I think the perogies used to be better."

"How can you remember that far back, Mom? That's twenty-seven years ago." His own memories of the event were fragmentary — the girl he'd been with, the suit he'd bought for the occasion, but little else. If he had known then that his own daughter would graduate from his high school, he would have been amazed and dismayed.

He spoke to the neighbour during the meal, and learned that he had moved away and then returned to town in recent years.

"We tried BC for a while," he said. "It was all right, too, as far as that goes. But then my wife died of cancer, and I moved back to take care of my mother, who was ninety-four at the time. After she died, I thought of going back to BC or moving to the city. But what do I want with city life? Lining up every morning with the golden-agers, waiting for the Wal-Mart to open so's I can get my fifty-five-plus discount. What kind of life is that?"

Everett nodded, thinking it was only ten years until he was fifty-five. Life had once been a long, steady climb, one goal achieved after another — education, a career, a house, a child. By forty, things had levelled out. He'd felt secure and confident, old enough to know what he was doing, and young enough to get it done. It was the best time of life, and he thought it would last.

But the ground under his feet had shifted. "All downhill from here" had become more than a worn cliché. His parents suddenly became elderly, and he began to feel at times, uncomfortably, that he was waiting for them to die. His own death, still perhaps forty years distant, was nonetheless real. He could see it now from where he stood.

The emcee was at the microphone, launching into a story about one of the grads.

"Shane was driving his Honda into Gravelbourg one night," he began, smiling broadly as if the audience already knew the story, "and a thunderstorm blew up and it started to rain hard. Pretty soon, the grid road got a little greasy, and when he came to a hill, Shane couldn't quite make the slope. Then he saw some bales off in the ditch, the square ones, and he got the idea — probably from Mr. Hendricks' physics class — he got the idea that a little added weight might help. So he tossed a couple bales up on his hood, and sure enough, the extra traction gave him just enough momentum to make the slope. And he didn't even have to stop to unload. Before he reached the top, the bales co-operated by sliding off the car, and he went on his merry way to town.

"Well, sometime early the next morning, Shane is on his way home from a night of partying in town. As it always seems to do in these parts, the rain had let up soon after it started, and now the road's dry and smooth, and it's almost time for chores. So he's got the Honda cranked up to about a hundred thirty clicks when he comes over a rise. And there on the road in front of him, right in his headlights, are those two, damn, bales!

The storyteller paused to make room for the laughter, then turned to look at the red-faced boy. "And what're you driving tonight, Shane? We haven't seen that Honda in a while."

More laughter, and then in a quieter, summing-up tone of voice: "Yes, folks, that little unfortunate incident gave 'Jap-scrap' a whole new meaning."

Everett laughed with the rest of them. But he found himself thinking, even as he laughed, that the story said too much that was true about life here, maybe about his own life. But what it said, he couldn't exactly be sure.

A HONDA PLAYED A ROLE in Aimee's story, too, a hopped-up CRX hatchback with oversized dual exhausts and darkly-tinted back windows. It was parked in the alley behind the house the night everything came to a head.

The year she turned fourteen, Aimee started drinking. Afraid they were losing control, Everett tried taking a hard line at first, insisting that as long as she lived under their roof she couldn't come home drunk. So she stopped coming home, disappearing for days at a time into a network of the homes of friends, and friends of friends. Susan and he had argued.

"Don't you see what you're doing?" she said, her mouth tight. "You're driving her away. This is her house too, and mine. As long as this is my home, this is Aimee's home. As long as she wants to come back here, no matter what she's been doing, I'm going to let her in."

He'd given in to her, and lapsed into long days and nights of numb, angry silence. While he pretended to be asleep, Susan would meet Aimee at the door and help her downstairs to her room.

There were good days, occasionally a good week. Aimee found a part-time job at a doughnut shop and liked it. At times she was disconcertingly honest, telling them about the all-night raves she'd gone to, and the drugs she'd tried. But the good times always ended in angry confrontation.

Something woke him at three a.m., and he found her at the doorway pulling on a jacket. He told her she was staying home.

"So what are you going to do, Dad?" she said, her face contorted with sarcasm. "Tie me to my bedpost?" She watched him as he tried to think of something to say. "I didn't think so."

She slammed the door behind her. He watched, helpless and furious, as she approached a car parked at the curb and got in.

It was the black Honda that night, and after that he noticed that it was the same car that showed up regularly. Aimee began to spend more time on the phone, and her moods seemed even more volatile. He found himself missing her predictable sullenness. Now she plunged from shrieking, giggling highs to tearful, black depths.

After Aimee came home one night, Susan took longer than usual to return to bed. When she did, she folded her pillow in two, and lay stiffly beside him.

"What's wrong?"

She hesitated. "This is a bad relationship Aimee's got herself into," she said finally.

"What did you expect, that she'd pick a nice responsible, church-going guy to get hammered with? At least she's consistent. Bad choices in every part of life."

Susan was angry. "Everett, shut up and listen for once. Quit sulking in your corner and get involved. I can't deal with this by myself."

He sat up and turned on the light.

"He's manipulative, controlling, jealous. He wants to know where she is all the time. Doesn't want her to spend time with her other friends."

"I can't see Aimee putting up with that," Everett said. "Whatever else she is, she certainly knows her own mind."

"She's not as tough as you think she is. She's scared, and there's a part of her that wants out, but it's hard. She thinks she loves him, she thinks he loves her. You know what it's like at that age."

"No," Everett said after a long silence. "I don't. I don't think it was ever like that for me."

"She showed me her bruises tonight," Susan said, her voice lowered, fragile. "She's really scared."

It was a moment or two before he understood what she was saying. Then anger came over him like a sudden fever. His hands tingled, his breathing became constricted. "If she doesn't dump him," he said, his voice trembling, "I'll make him wish she had."

She touched his arm. "Everett, it's bad enough, don't go making it worse. If you lose your head, she's probably going to defend him more. Give her some space. Trust her to make the right decision."

"Why should I?"

"Because it's the only way that has any chance of working."

Two weeks later, Susan told him that Aimee had ended the relationship. Aimee seemed subdued for a few days afterward, sad but relieved.

Everett felt that a weight had lifted from their lives, but the feeling didn't last. Before long, they noticed that Aimee was withdrawn and agitated. They overheard angry telephone conversations, and one evening she left the house abruptly and rode off in the Honda.

"Will this ever be over?" Everett asked Susan. "I just want to have some kind of normal life."

In less than an hour, Aimee was home again.

"He won't leave me alone," she said, in tears. "He's phoning me all the time, and following me. He says he's going to hurt himself really bad if I don't go out with him again."

"Don't do it, Aimee," Everett said. "Please."

"I'm not that stupid, Dad."

They started to screen her calls, and Susan drove her to and from school. But Aimee told them that she had seen his car close to the school, and when she went shopping with her friends, he'd shown up suddenly and confronted her at the mall.

Lying awake one night in June, Everett heard the harsh blat from the exhaust of an idling car. The sound seemed to be coming from the alley. He got up quickly, dressed, and slipped out the back door. He picked up an old axe handle from under the deck, and headed for the back gate, his pulse beating hard in his ears and temples.

It was the Honda, its back end toward him, just a few yards distant. He lunged toward the driver's side. In the instant before he jerked the door open, he saw a dimly-lit face turned toward the house.

"You stay away from her." His voice had lost its strength. He reached for the boy and he saw him recoil, clutching for the gear-shift. The engine revved up suddenly, and as the car pulled away from him Everett swung the axe handle blindly. A hole opened in the back window, and he heard fragments of glass scattering on the pavement. The car reached the end of the alley, squealed onto the street, and was gone.

He was trembling, the axe handle still in his hand, when he woke Susan to tell her what had happened.

"I don't think we can take much more of this," Everett said. "Another second and I could have really hurt that kid. Something has to change."

Aimee appeared silently at the open door of their room, her eyes wide and face pale.

"I'm sorry," she said, and sat on the edge of the bed next to Susan. She started to cry, and Susan held her.

"I think we should call the police," Everett suggested. "We can get a restraining order to keep him away from you."

"Do you think that will work?" Susan asked him. "Would that keep him away?"

Everett shook his head. "I don't know — it's the only option I can think of."

Susan stroked Aimee's arm. "We're at our wits' end, Aimee. What do you want us to do?"

"I don't want you to do anything," she said in a small voice. "I just want a new life. I want to go someplace where nobody can find me."

"How about my mom and dad's?" Everett said. "For the summer at least. School's over next week, and we can all keep quiet about where you've gone."

To their surprise, Aimee agreed. By the end of that first summer, she had made a few friends, and was still afraid to come back to the city, even though none of them had seen her boyfriend for months. So she started grade eleven in a small town high school. Despite a few complaints from Everett's parents, and some from Aimee about rural life, she did well in school that year and settled into a circle of friends.

After grade eleven, she came home for a few weeks during the summer. But she hadn't kept up her friendships in the city, and felt lonely and out of place. During a family camping trip, she told her parents that she wanted to go back to live with her grandparents.

"I miss my friends," she told them.

"What about grade twelve?" Susanna asked.

Aimee was silent for a moment. "It's just one more year," she said, "and I want to graduate with my friends."

Susanna looked at Everett, and he nodded.

"If it's what you want, and if Grandma and Grandpa can put up with you," Susanna said, "then it's okay with us."

It's really not okay with me, Everett thought. But it was probably the best they could do, so he said nothing.

WHEN HE FELT THE FIRST hesitation of the Cherokee's motor, he shifted into neutral. He shut off the ignition to preserve the last of the fuel, hoping it would start more easily if he didn't run it dry. He coasted toward an approach he could see ahead on the right, and then braked and turned off the road. He switched off the lights, then stepped out into the semi-darkness of early dawn.

By the glow of the eastern sky, he saw a barbed wire gate in front of him, and beyond that what seemed to be unbroken native grassland. He could smell the sage and cow manure. He lifted the loop of wire from the top of the post at one end of the gate, lowered it, and stepped into the field.

The sky was brightening perceptibly, but the ground was deeply shadowed. He felt his way forward. Behind him, he heard the tick of the motor as it cooled, and around him the rustle of the breeze through the stiff grass. He felt a coarse, springy growth in the darkness beneath his feet, and he crouched and spread his hands over the low fronds. Juniper. It seemed to be growing everywhere here in the light soil, thriving despite drought and four-wheel drives. He checked for a dry spot and sat down, facing back toward the road. The surface of the juniper was prickly, but it was surprisingly comfortable. He could feel clusters of its tiny berries under his hands, imagined their pale sky-blue about to emerge with the morning light.

He remembered telling Susanna that it wasn't what Aimee did or didn't do that hurt the most. It was the void that opened between them, the feeling of being shut out of her life, maybe forever.

It wouldn't be forever. He'd realized that soon after she moved out. But there were two years of her life — two years of their lives together, the three of them in the same house, the routines of eating and joking and looking at the same television screen — two years they could never get back. He felt the heft of those lost days now, the tangible weight of her absence.

Sitting here, he could admit at last that nothing would ever make up for that loss. There was nothing to do now but grieve and let it go, nothing to do but sit in the darkness and wait.

MADELEINE GREENWAY

Born in 1953, Eric Greenway was raised on a farm near Hanna, Alberta. In 1993, he won a Saskatchewan Writers Guild literary award for his story, "The House of the Lamp," which appears in this collection. That story was subsequently broadcast on CBC Radio, and a number of others have appeared in the Smoky Peace anthologies, published in Grande Prairie, Alberta. Eric is one of the founding members of Notes from the Underground writers' group, whose members have offered invaluable critiques of earlier drafts of these stories. He has lived in Regina since 1983, and is presently employed with the Canadian Diabetes Association. Eric is married and has three daughters. *The Darkness Beneath All Things* is his first book.